I dedicate this book to my incredible son, Cree,
and my lovely and supportive husband, Cory.
—Tia

To my entire family—my mother, Darlene; father,
Timothy; my brothers, Tahj and Tavior; sister, Tia;
husband, Adam; son, Aden; and daughter, Ariah.
—Tamera

1
CAITLYN

"DID YOU GUYS ever hear of the Birthday Paradox?" Liam asked through a mouthful of half-chewed rice.

I added another dab of hot sauce to my burrito. It was Tex-Mex Thursday, and even though I'd only been at Aura Middle School for a little over three weeks, I'd already learned to ask the cafeteria ladies for extra spice. Nothing bums me out like a bland burrito.

"The birthday what?" I said.

"The Birthday Paradox." Bianca didn't bother looking up from her book, which she was reading between bites of food. "Yeah, I've heard of it."

"Not me." I shrugged. "What is it?"

"It's an equation that proves if you have twenty-three random people in a room, there's a fifty-percent chance at least two of them will share the same birthday," Liam said. "It's a probability theory."

Typical Liam—he was supersmart, but unlike most supersmart people, he assumed everyone was just as smart as him. It was sweet, though occasionally confusing—sort of like Liam O'Day himself. I considered myself lucky that he'd been the first friend I'd made after moving to Aura, Texas. He'd introduced me to Bianca Ramos, who was just as nice, though a lot quieter.

"Twenty-three people, huh?" I capped the hot sauce. "In my house, all we need is two people to make it a hundred-percent chance—as long as those two people are me and Cassie."

Liam let out his snorty laugh, flipping his messy red hair off his forehead. "Good one, Caitlyn!"

Bianca glanced at me. "It must be weird sharing your birthday with a twin."

"Not really." I shrugged. "I mean, not to us. We're used to it, you know?"

"So what are you going to do to celebrate the big 1-2?" Liam asked.

"Not sure yet. My birthday kind of snuck up on me this year." I poked a black bean back into my burrito. "Cass and I usually throw a party together or something, but we haven't even talked about it yet."

My gaze wandered across the crowded cafeteria. My sister was sitting at the big table dead smack in the middle of the room, where the most popular sixth graders hung out.

That was new. At least sort of. For the first week or so after we'd moved to this tiny town, Cassie had seemed determined to live up to the *lone* in "Lone Star State." No friends, no fun, no way. She was that sure we'd be moving back to San Antonio once our mother realized how lame this place was. It had never seemed to occur to her that Mom might actually *like* living in a small town. Or that I might, too. Or that she might not totally hate it herself.

Then again, I wasn't too shocked by her reaction. The move had been a surprise for both of us, and Cassie didn't always handle surprises well. Oh, don't get me wrong—we were both used to moving. Mom had been in the army since before we were born, which meant we'd lived all over the country.

But we'd been in San Antonio for almost three years—a record for us. When Mom retired from the military and went to the police academy, we'd figured the city was home sweet home for good. Things didn't turn out that way, though. There weren't any open spots on the force there, and Mom had landed a job in Aura instead.

I'd tried to make the best of things from the start. It's just what I do. Cassie? Not so much. Our mom says she was born looking for the dark cloud behind the silver lining. She could be stubborn as a three-legged mule, too. And she'd been certain from the start that living in Aura was going to be about as pleasant as wet socks. To be honest, I still wasn't sure what had changed her mind. But I was glad she'd finally decided to fit in. And not at all surprised that she'd wormed her way into the popular crowd lickety-split.

Liam's gaze followed mine over to Cassie. "Do you share your presents, too?" he asked.

"No way," I said. "Good thing. Cassie and I don't exactly have the same taste, if you hadn't noticed."

Not anymore, anyway. Once upon a time, we'd loved being twins. We'd been best friends and done everything together. We'd even dressed alike as often as Mom would let us.

When had that changed? I couldn't quite recall. These days we still looked alike, with matching big brown eyes and skinny legs. But everything else about us was different.

Okay, wait. Maybe we did have one other thing in common lately. One *major* thing.

"So what about your dad?" Liam asked. "Does he visit or send you stuff on your birthday?"

I blinked, startled. "My dad?"

Bianca nudged Liam. "Don't be so nosy," she

muttered. "We don't even know if . . ." She glanced at me and shrugged. "You never talk about your father."

True enough. "Yeah, sorry. I probably should've said something sooner." I tried to sound normal. "He died years ago. When Cass and I were babies."

"Oh!" Liam's eyes widened. "I just figured your folks were divorced like mine. Sorry."

"Yeah, me, too," Bianca said softly, not quite meeting my eyes.

For a second she looked really sad and sort of distant, which was kind of weird. As far as I knew, both her parents were still totally alive and happily married right there in Aura, Texas. Maybe she was thinking about a grandparent who'd passed on or something. Whatever—I wasn't going to pry. Especially since I didn't want them to ask me any more questions either. Like how my dad died, or what he'd done for a living, or what he was like. Little stuff like that. None of which I knew the answer to. Weird, right?

But that was how it was. For as long as I could remember, our mom had refused to talk about him.

No matter what we asked, all she'd say was, "We'll discuss it when you're older." For some reason, she'd made up her mind that the whole topic was off-limits. And when Deidre Waters set her mind to something, it stayed set. Period, full stop, and woe to the girl who tried to push her.

Just about all Cassie and I knew about our dad was that his name was John Thompson, and that Mom met him while she was stationed overseas when she first joined the army. We also knew that he was white, with sandy hair and a square jaw. But only because Cassie talked me into sneaking into Mom's room when we were six or seven and peeking at the wedding photo packed away in a big box on the top shelf that we were *absolutely not* supposed to touch. Mom never found out about that. At least we don't think she did. Although the next time Cass tried to find that box, it was gone, so who knows.

Anyway, since Mom wouldn't tell us anything, Cass and I made up all kinds of wild, crazy, romantic stuff about our dad. Like that he was an international spy who saved the world on a regular basis.

Or a pirate who robbed from the rich and gave to the poor. Or a movie star who was always off shooting fabulous films in exotic locations. But lately, we didn't talk to each other about our father much. What was the point?

"I'll have to get with Cass about next weekend's party plans," I told my friends, taking a bite of my burrito as I changed the subject. "Whatever we're doing, y'all are invited for sure."

I hoped Cassie was okay with that. She seemed to think my new friends were nerds. So what if they were? I liked them, and that was all that mattered.

Liam stabbed a stray bean with his fork. "Maybe you guys should do a movie party. You could make it a monster-movie theme and tell people to come in costume. I still have this awesome Godzilla suit from last Halloween."

I grinned, imagining what Cassie would say to that idea. As tough as she liked to act, scary movies freaked her out. Even cheesy monster ones.

"I'll take it under advisement," I told Liam, scooping up all the hot sauce that had dripped out of my burrito. "Any other ideas?"

"There's a new minigolf place over the other side of Six Oaks."

. "Hmm." Miniature golf actually sounded kind of fun. I made a mental note to mention it to Cass. "Okay, that's another one for the list. Next?"

As usual, Liam was full of ideas, and we spent the rest of lunch discussing party plans. Bianca had less to say, though she did veto Liam's suggestion of an insect cuisine cook-off—apparently he'd seen something on TV about how nutritious and ecologically correct it was to turn our six-legged friends into a major part of our diet.

I had to agree with Bianca on the bug thing. Otherwise I didn't care what we did as long as everyone had fun. I couldn't wait to figure out a plan with Cassie—just like old times.

The thought made me smile. That was one good thing about the crazy stuff that had been happening to me and Cassie lately. It had brought us together again, just when I was afraid she'd drifted so far away I barely knew her anymore.

As I followed my friends out of the cafeteria, someone grabbed my arm. It was Ms. Xavier. She was my homeroom teacher and also taught social studies. With her wild, wavy hair, jangling bracelets, and flowing boho skirts, she stood out among the other teachers like a peacock among chickens. Her style wasn't really my thing, but I had to admire her for following her own drummer.

"Cassie Waters!" she exclaimed in her loud, enthusiastic voice. "I wanted to talk to you before— oh!" Her kohl-lined eyes widened, and she laughed. "Sorry, Caitlyn. I thought you were your twin for a second."

I smiled politely. Cass and I used to get mistaken for each other all the time back in the days when we dressed alike and wore our hair the same way. Now? Not so much. Most people caught on quickly that Cass was the sister who was always decked out in the latest fashions, while I was the one who went for a more comfortable, classic look. But like I said, Ms. Xavier's personal style was so far out there that she probably didn't really notice the difference.

"I think Cassie already left." I hoped Ms. Xavier wasn't looking for Cass because of some kind of problem. Social studies had never been one of my sister's best subjects.

"It's all right; she has my class next," the teacher said. "I'll catch up with her there. But as long as I have you, Caitlyn, I want to talk to you, too."

"Um, okay." I hoped she didn't have too much to say. I had to head to math, and Ms. Church was tough on tardiness. "What is it?"

"Have you decided on a topic for your research project yet?" she asked.

Every sixth grader was supposed to do a written and oral report on a topic related to US history, society, or culture. Bianca already had her project on the Civil War half done, though most people were still in the planning stages since the project wasn't due for over a month.

"Um, not yet, but I'm narrowing it down," I said. "I was thinking about doing something on Lewis and Clark, or maybe the Alamo, since I used to live near—"

"Great, great," she broke in, nodding like a bob-blehead. "But before you settle on anything, I had a thought. Twins are such an interesting aspect of human society. Maybe you could do your project on well-known American twins? For instance, there are those twin astronauts, or the former mayor of San Antonio and his twin who became a congress-man, and I'm sure there are others." She squeezed my elbow. "Perhaps you could even look into whether being a twin helped lead to their success."

"What do you mean?" I asked, a little confused. "How would being a twin make a difference?"

Her smile broadened. "Well, I was thinking about everything I've read and heard about twins having special powers and thought it would be fascinating to look into that aspect of things, you know?"

I gulped, suddenly very aware of her hand on my arm. Special powers? She didn't know the half of it!

It had all started about six months earlier. I began getting visions of people when I touched them—whether it was a hug, a handshake, or just a brief pat on the arm—and these visions came true. It didn't happen every time I touched someone, but when it did, the person I was touching would fade away and be replaced by a different vision of that person. For instance, one time I'd been talking to Cassie when I suddenly got a vision of her coming home with an A on a test. And then a couple of days later, it had actually happened.

The first few times, I'd thought it was a coincidence—just a weird daydream or something. It was only after we moved to Aura that I discovered Cassie was having these visions, too, and we realized we were seeing the future.

If that didn't qualify as a special power, what did?

If Ms. Xavier noticed my reaction, she didn't show it. She was smiling at me. I returned the smile uncertainly. "I'll think about it, I guess," I said.

"Good, good!" She beamed at me. "And, listen, if you and Cassie want to work together on it, I'd be happy to give you special permission. I know you two girls are in separate classes, and it's supposed to be an individual project, but it would be much more powerful if both of you contributed, hmm?"

"Oh. Um, okay." I wasn't sure what else to say. Being the only twins at AMS was kind of weird— almost like being celebrities or something. At our old school in San Antonio, there had been two other sets in our grade alone, plus some triplets in the eighth grade. Here? We were a novelty. It had been obvious since day one, when Ms. Xavier had introduced me to the class and then started babbling about twins having voodoo powers or something.

Ms. Xavier patted my arm. "If you're interested, I could help you come up with some ways to make the project more personal."

"Personal?" I echoed.

She nodded. "There are numerous studies on nature versus nurture, of course. But I was just reading about a much more interesting experiment involving the telepathic bond between twins, and I thought—"

Just then, a kid rushed over. "Ms. X, I need to talk to you," he said. "I lost my textbook, but it's totally not my fault. Jason grabbed it away right when we were near the pond, and . . ."

Whew! That was my cue to escape. Muttering a quick "Bye," I took off down the hall.

2

CASSIE

"COMING, CASSIE?"

I glanced up from stuffing my books into my messenger bag. Megan March was smiling at me from the doorway of our classroom, her books already neatly tucked away in her designer tote.

Slipping a stray pen in on top of my textbooks, I picked up my bag. "Coming."

I fell into step beside her as we left the classroom. A couple of Megan's other friends scurried after us, chattering at each other about tonight's homework assignment. Their names were Emily and Abby, though I mostly just thought of them as the minions. Not to their faces, of course—I wasn't a total cretin. They were nice enough, just sort of bland and interchangeable.

In any case, I wasn't interested in discussing homework. School was over for the day, and I wanted to think about something more interesting.

And as it happened, something more interesting was right in front of me. Brayden Diaz was swinging down the hall on his crutches, talking to a friend. And looking positively adorable, as always.

I tried not to stare. I wasn't sure exactly what I thought about Brayden just yet. Until I figured it out, nobody needed to know I had any thoughts about him at all.

"So what are you doing this weekend?" I asked Megan, carefully keeping my voice casual. I'd only been friends with her for a week or two and couldn't take anything for granted yet. Popularity was fragile

TWINTUITION: DOUBLE TROUBLE

when you were the new kid. Not that Megan ever had to worry about that. She was practically Aura royalty—her mom was the mayor, her uncle the chief of police, and her whole family had lived in this town basically forever.

It didn't hurt that she was pretty and blond, with a sense of style rivaled only by my own. My gaze flicked down to her cute jeweled sandals, and I wondered if we were good enough friends yet for me to ask to borrow them.

"I'm not sure yet," Megan said. "Football game tomorrow afternoon, obviously."

"Obviously," I echoed. Football was king in Aura, like most everywhere in Texas, and our middle school team, the Aura Armadillos, was undefeated. Although things were looking dicey now that the star quarterback was out for the rest of the season with a broken leg.

My gaze zipped forward. Brayden was high-fiving some of his friends from the football team, who'd been waiting for him at the far end of the hall. Brayden spent so much time with Biff, Brent, and Buzz that everyone called the four of them the B Boys. I tried to pretend I wasn't watching as Brent smacked Brayden on the shoulder, then Brayden laughed and hit Buzz on the leg with one of his crutches. They were still goofing off as they disappeared around the corner.

I closed my eyes for a second, remembering Brayden's hand gripping mine as he writhed on the ground in pain after his leg had snapped in a bad tackle last weekend. It wasn't something I could forget, especially since I'd seen it twice: Once when it had happened, and once a few days *before* it had happened.

My eyes flew open as a nasty voice came from right behind me: "Wake up, Waters. You're blocking traffic."

I glanced around just in time to see Gabe Campbell shoot me a poisonous glare as he stomped past, his battered cowboy boots clomping on the floor.

"Oops, looks like someone's still mad at you," Megan commented.

I just nodded. Gabe's uncle was the reason Mom

had a job here in Aura. Sort of. Chuck Campbell had been on the force for years—and he'd been embezzling money from the town almost as long. After he was fired, he'd held a grudge against Mom for taking his job—and Gabe seemed to be holding a grudge against Cassie and me for the same reason.

Megan and I continued down the hall to her locker, still trailed by the minions. Lavender Adams was already there, leaning against the wall, picking at her fingernails.

She looked up when she heard us coming. "Hey," she said to Megan.

Okay, technically she said it to all of us. But her hazel eyes barely registered me before settling on Megan and the minions. I tried not to let it bother me. Lavender hadn't accepted me into the group as quickly as Megan and the others had. Sometimes she almost felt like a friend, and other times? Well, not so much. But I wasn't too worried. Most people liked me once they got to know me, and I was sure Lavender was no exception.

"We were just talking about weekend plans," I

told her with a friendly smile.

"Way to plan ahead, Cassie." Lavender shrugged. "It's only Thursday; we still have a whole 'nother day of school to survive first."

Megan laughed. "All the more reason to think about something fun, right?" She clicked open her locker and checked her reflection in the mirror she'd stuck on the door. "Unfortunately I don't think I can do anything on Saturday. Mom's having some kind of dinner party for a bunch of boring town businesspeople, and I'm supposed to help her get ready."

"Bummer," I said. "I hope your mom doesn't have you scheduled for anything *next* Saturday, though. Because it's my birthday, and you're all invited to help me celebrate."

"Your birthday? Really?" Megan glanced at me. "I didn't know that was coming up."

I shrugged, not bothering to remind her that up until a week or so ago, she wouldn't have cared. "Yeah," I said. "With the move and all, I haven't had a chance to make any plans."

"I can fix that." Lavender suddenly looked a lot friendlier. "Party time!"

I laughed and high-fived her. "Pretty much what I was thinking."

"What kind of party are you having, Cassie?" one of the minions asked.

"I haven't thought about it yet. Any ideas?"

"Sure," Lavender said immediately. "Boy-girl party, cool DJ. Finger food."

"Dancing?" a minion said.

"Naturally," Lavender replied.

Megan smiled. "Sounds like the perfect place to wear that cute new dress I got when we were shopping last week."

"Totally," Lavender agreed. She glanced at me. "Make sure to tell the DJ there should be lots of slow songs, right?"

The second minion giggled. "Perfect!"

Before I could say anything, Lavender suddenly frowned.

"Wait," she said. "Don't you live over on Granite Street?" She wrinkled her nose. "Maybe you should have the party somewhere else."

Okay, obnoxious. But she had a point. Our new place in Aura was so tiny that Caitlyn and I had to share a bedroom, something we hadn't done since we were six. At first we'd both been horrified. I'm kind of type A when it comes to cleaning and organizing, while Cait's more like type P, for *pigsty*. But so far it had actually been okay. At least mostly.

"My cousin had her Sweet Sixteen at that big hotel in Six Oaks," one of the minions said. "The ballroom there is really swank!"

Megan nodded, looking interested. "Did she get it catered?"

Yikes. This was getting out of control.

"Hang on," I said. "Don't forget, it's my sister's birthday, too."

"Your sister?" Lavender's nose wrinkled even more dramatically. I wanted to warn her that her face might freeze that way, but it didn't seem like the right moment.

"Yes, my *twin* sister, remember?" I shrugged. "Whatever we do, I have to run it by her."

And call me crazy, but I had the feeling Caitlyn wasn't going to go for Lav's idea of a swanky slow-dance party. Not that it mattered. I definitely didn't have the funds to throw a party like that, and I doubted I'd be able to talk Mom into it either.

Lavender looked unimpressed. "Anyway," she said, "what do you guys think about our chances against the Tigers tomorrow? You know, with Brayden out of commission . . ."

We were still talking about the football team a few minutes later when we headed for the exit. Lavender pushed open the heavy front door, letting a blast of AC out with a whoosh.

"Ugh," I said as the late afternoon heat smacked me in the face. "Remind me to move to Alaska soon, okay?"

Megan laughed. "Funny, Cass."

"I'm not joking," I said, smirking to show that I was. At least sort of. "This kind of weather makes my hair go all kinky. It would only be tolerable if I had a pool."

Lavender shrugged. "Megan has one."

I wasn't surprised. Megan was totally the type of person whose house would have a pool. Probably a fancy one with a waterfall and a slide.

"Yeah." Megan dug her lip gloss out of her purse. "Normally my parents would have shut it down for the winter by now. But my dad keeps saying they'll wait until it gets cold."

"Hey, there's your sister, Cassie," one of the minions said. "Maybe we should go talk to her about your party."

"No," I said quickly. I could only imagine how Cait would react to my friends bombarding her with their ideas. "I just remembered my mom wants us home early today. But don't worry, I'll talk to her. See you!"

I rushed off toward Caitlyn, who was waiting for me near the flagpole. I'd barely seen her all day. Aura Middle School was so small that the entire sixth grade was divided into only two sections—green and gold, named after the school colors. Megan, Emily, Abby, and I were in the gold section. So was Brayden. Cait was in green with her dorky friends, along with Lavender and the other three B Boys.

"Hi," I said when I reached my sister. "Where's the nerd patrol?"

She frowned slightly. "If you mean Liam and Bianca, they already left."

Oops. So much for starting our birthday party discussion on the right foot. Still, with only a little over a week to make plans, I couldn't wait for a better moment. Besides, Cait wasn't the type to hold a grudge.

"I've been thinking about our birthday," I said as we started walking.

She brightened. "Me, too. Liam told me there's a new minigolf place in Six Oaks. Should we go there? We could each invite a few friends, maybe get pizza after."

"Minigolf and pizza?" I shrugged. "That'd be perfect if we were turning eight, not twelve. We only have one more year until we're officially teenagers, right? It's time to stop with the baby parties and do something fun. Maybe at night, with dancing. My friends are totally willing to help us plan it."

"Are you kidding?" Caitlyn said. "Mom isn't going to let us have some teenagery dance party. I mean, have you met her?"

I frowned. "She owes us one. She made us move here, remember? I'm sure she'll be reasonable."

Cait was starting to get a stubborn expression that I didn't like. "Well, I don't want that kind of party," she said. "We're not teenagers yet. Why rush it?"

I rolled my eyes. Why hadn't I predicted this? Oh, wait—I had. Caitlyn and I used to have a ton in common, but over the past few years she'd turned into someone I barely recognized. Even those stupid visions we'd both started having showed how different we've become—all of Cait's seemed to show good stuff happening to people, while mine showed bad or horrible or unpleasant stuff. Totally unfair, right?

"Whatever," I said. "It's way too hot to argue about it. We'll deal with it later."

"Fine," she replied.

We trudged the rest of the way home in silence. As she opened the front door, Caitlyn glanced at me.

"It's not that I don't want to have a party," she said. "I just think we need to talk about the details a little more."

"Okay." This was a little more promising. I could work with this. "Maybe we can compromise. The first thing is to figure out where to have the party." My eyes swept the place as I stepped inside. The house was so small that I could hear the squeak of the shower turning off down the hall. "Definitely not here."

"Why not?" Cait looked around, too. "It's not like we're inviting the whole school, right? I'm okay with keeping the guest list small."

Just then Mom emerged from the bathroom in a cloud of steam, one towel wrapped around her body and another around her head. "What are you girls talking about?" she asked.

"Our birthday," Cait said.

"Coming up next weekend, or did you forget?" I added, "That doesn't give us much time to plan the party, but—"

"Are you sure you want a party this year?" Mom

interrupted. She fiddled with the edge of her towel, not really looking at either of us. "I was thinking the three of us could go out for a nice dinner. Or maybe cook something here at home. We haven't had brisket in a while."

I shook my head. "No way! You only turn twelve once, right?"

"I can't believe you two are almost twelve already. It seems like just yesterday you were learning to walk." Mom shook her head, looking kind of wistful, which so wasn't like her. She's hardly the sappy, sentimental type. She's not the twitchy type either, though she was acting a little that way right now.

Caitlyn stepped over and put an arm around her shoulders. "Oh, Mom, we . . ."

Her voice trailed off. Suddenly she sort of stiffened, and her eyes went all weird and distant. Uh-oh. I instantly guessed what that meant. She was having a vision!

"C'mon, Cait, leave her alone," I said, yanking her away from Mom.

As soon as they weren't touching anymore, Cait's face cleared. She still looked a little confused, though.

Luckily Mom didn't seem to notice as she checked her watch. "We'll have to talk more about your birthday later. I need to get dressed for work or I'll be late."

She disappeared back down the hallway, toward her room. I stared at Caitlyn. "Let me guess," I said. "Vision?"

"Uh-huh." Cait blinked a few times, then took a deep breath. "Caught me by surprise. Tell you in a sec."

I knew how she felt. It always took a few seconds to go back to normal again after a vision. If you could call someone who saw the future *normal*.

"I was really hoping this would stop," I muttered. "Preferably before our birthday."

"Doubtful." Caitlyn collapsed onto the sofa. "Remember that website I found? An article on there said there's some family in England where each member starts getting visions around the time they turn twelve."

Caitlyn had been intrigued by the whole vision thing from the start. She'd done a bunch of research online and even posted a question on some wacka-doodle paranormal message board. Me? I didn't want to learn anything about our visions; I just wanted them to go away. If her research helped us figure out how to make that happen, I was all for it.

"That reminds me. Did you ever hear anything back from that crazy website?" I asked.

"I didn't tell you?" Cait sat up and stared at me. "When I checked the site again, the whole thread had been removed."

"Removed? What do you mean?"

Before she could answer, the doorbell rang. "Could you get that?" Mom's muffled voice rang out from the back of the house.

"Got it!" I hollered, already heading for the door.

When I swung it open, a delivery guy was stand-ing there. "Package for Waters?" he said, holding out a large, flat box covered in colorful foreign stamps.

I didn't answer for a second. I couldn't.

Because this wasn't the first time I'd seen that exact same package.

3

CAITLYN

"WHO IS IT?" I asked when Cassie didn't reappear right away.

I stepped onto the front stoop, glancing from my sister to the deliveryman. Then I gasped when I saw the package he was holding. My mind flashed to a vision I'd had last week—one we'd both had. It had showed Cass and me standing right here on our front step, holding a package. Holding *this* package.

"Is that for us?" I said, grabbing it from the guy. "Thanks."

"Sure." He tipped his hat, then hurried back toward his truck.

I grabbed Cass and yanked her inside. "Oh my gosh!" I hissed.

"I know, right?" Her eyes were wide and freaked out.

I glanced at the package. It was addressed in tidy, formal handwriting to Misses Caitlyn and Cassandra Waters. The stamps were from a mish-mash of foreign places—Germany, the UK, France, even one from Singapore.

"There's no return address," I said. "I wonder who it's from."

"One way to find out." She grabbed it from me and clawed at the tape.

"Wait!" I suddenly remembered something. "This could be important. Up until now, everything I've seen in my visions has showed something good happening to someone, and everything you've seen has been, you know . . ."

"Bad," Cassie finished with a slight frown.

For some reason, Cassie seemed to take it personally that she'd been seeing bad stuff so far. "But listen, this proves that was all just a coincidence, right? Because this time we both saw the same thing, and how can getting this package be good *and* bad?"

"Maybe someone sent you a birthday present and forgot to put mine in, too," Cassie joked. "Anyway, it's addressed to us, so let's open it already!"

She opened the package and slid out a flat, smaller wooden box. Lifting the lid, she revealed a small leather-bound book, its cover soft and worn with age. Beside it was a cream-colored, expensive-looking envelope and a tarnished silver pendant on a long chain.

"Cool necklace." Cassie picked up the pendant and dangled it for a better look. It was shaped like a fancy key, with an eye-shaped handle that had a star where the pupil should be.

Meanwhile I opened the envelope and pulled out what was inside. I glanced at Cassie just in time to see her slide the pendant on over her head.

"What?" she said at my look. "I'm sure this is for me. Is that a card?"

"More like a letter." I skimmed the first few lines and gasped. "You're not going to believe this! Listen."

I started to read:

"Dear Caitlyn and Cassandra, I hope it is not a complete surprise to hear from me, your grandmother, though I have not seen you since soon after your birth. I have, however, thought of you too many times since your dear father left us, and have often wished you could be here with me. However, I have honored your mother's wishes to remain apart from you—until now. With your twelfth birthday approaching rapidly, I know at least one of you must be experiencing the beginning stages of the Sight. That is why I have made the effort to locate you and send you this package. I am sure you must have questions about the family legacy, and the enclosed volume will answer many of them. This is very important, for without learning to manage your powers, you could—"

"What's that?" Mom's voice interrupted in mid-sentence.

I spun around. She was standing right behind me, dressed in her police uniform. Before I knew what was happening, she grabbed the letter out of my hand. As she read the beginning, her expression darkened.

"I see," she said. "I'll take this, too." She snatched the leather-bound book out of Cassie's hand.

"Hey!" Cass protested. "That was sent to us—Cait and me. Our names are on the box and everything."

"Yes," I said, still trying to take in what I'd just read. "It's from our—our grandmother."

Cassie nodded. "And it sure didn't sound like Maw Maw Jean either," she added. "It's got to be from our father's mom, right?"

"That's enough," Mom said. "This is a mistake, and that's the end of it."

She'd slipped into what we called her scarymama voice—the tone that brooked no argument. But why? We hadn't done anything wrong.

"But—" I began.

"That letter—" Cassie said at the same time.

Mom swept past us, her face twisted into an expression I couldn't quite figure out. She looked angry, yes—but also really freaked out. And that freaked *me* out. Mom was about the coolest cucumber on the planet.

"Hey, where are you going?" Cassie cried. Mom charged toward the door, pausing just long enough to grab her purse from the bench. She stuffed the book and letter inside.

"To work," Mom replied in a clipped voice without turning around.

I winced as the door slammed behind her hard enough to shake the house. "What was that all about?" I exclaimed. "I can't believe she took our stuff and left!"

"Not all of it." Cassie touched the necklace, which she was still wearing. "Guess she didn't notice this."

"I can't believe we have a grandmother we never knew about," I said. "And she seemed to know about our visions, too. At least I bet that's what she meant by 'the Sight.'"

"Yeah." Cassie frowned, fiddling with the key-shaped pendant. "Mom seemed to know who it was from, though. And she didn't like it."

"The letter said our grandmother was honoring Mom's wishes to stay away from us," I recalled.

Cassie bit her lip, staring at me with troubled brown eyes. "So does that mean Mom knew about this weirdo twin superpower thing all along? And didn't tell us?"

"We don't know that for sure," I said quickly. "Anyway, at least we know we're not going crazy, right? Sounds like this Sight thing is something that's passed down in our dad's family or something. Sort of like those Lockwood people I read about on that website."

"Yeah. Speaking of which, what vision did you get from Mom before?"

I'd almost forgotten about the image that had hit me when I'd put my arm around Mom a few minutes earlier.

"Actually," I said. "It showed Mom holding hands with a—a guy."

"What guy?"

I shrugged. "He looked sort of like our dad, actually," I told her. "At least as much as I can remember about that wedding picture. He was a nice-looking white guy with light brown hair and a square chin."

"Huh," Cassie said. "I thought these visions were supposed to show the future, not the past. Or are you branching out now?"

"I don't think it was the past. Mom looked pretty much like she does now, and the guy was around her age. It's probably just someone who looks a little like our dad."

"Guess this means Mom is finally going to start dating again," Cassie said. "And apparently she's got a type."

"Yeah." Something about the vision bothered me. Was it the idea of my mother going out on a date? She hadn't really done that much, especially in the last few years. "Do you think it's—you know, unhealthy? Her dating someone who looks so much like her dead husband, I mean."

"Probably not a big deal." Cassie shrugged. "I mean, you only see good stuff, right?"

"But the package . . ."

"Think about it, girl," Cassie said. "The package really did turn out to be good *and* bad, right? It's good that it came, because now we know there's someone out there who knows what's happening to us."

"But it's bad that Mom saw it and took it away."

"Yeah." Cassie paused, shooting me a sidelong glance. "Anyway, good or not, it's weird to think about Mom dating someone new. Did she look happy in the vision?"

"Yes," I said. "Yes, she did. She was smiling. Oh! And I forgot to say there was a Christmas tree in the background. I couldn't really see much else, though."

"Christmas? Really? Okay, that's ages away. Let's not stress over it yet." Cassie touched the necklace, a determined glint in her eye. "Right now, we have more urgent things to deal with—starting with how we're going to get our stuff back."

4
CASSIE

FRIDAYS WERE ALWAYS rough. The weekend was right there, so close you could practically taste it, but our teachers expected us to sit through hours and hours of superboring classes before we could escape. Wretched!

This particular Friday was more awful than usual. I couldn't focus in my first two classes. All I could think about was that mysterious package— and the way Mom had gone nuts about it.

The worst part? She was still refusing to tell us

why. It was like our dad all over again. For years, she'd put off our questions by saying she'd tell us someday. But "someday" hadn't come yet, and she was still keeping mum.

Now here we were, with our first hint in forever about that side of the family. And once again, Mom was stonewalling us. Talk about unfair! I mean, she'd always been strict, running our household like some kind of military camp, at least in some ways. When she said jump, Cait and I were supposed to jump. No questions asked. Not even, "How high?"

But that had never seemed like a big deal. Because I'd always trusted her before. Always been sure she had our best interests at heart, even if she sometimes had a funny way of showing it.

Now? I wasn't so sure. Was it possible she'd known all along that Cait and I would end up with these freaky visions? Was it possible she knew—and hadn't even bothered to warn us? That she'd just sat back, letting us think we were going psycho, when all along she could have helped us understand?

Those sorts of questions kept swirling around in

my head all morning. Things weren't any better by the time I headed to the library for study hall.

Megan fell into step beside me. "Want to look at magazines, or do you have to finish the social studies homework?" she asked as we pushed through the library's glass doors. "Abs and Ems are frantic because they both forgot that geography worksheet is due today."

"Huh?" I blinked at her.

"Magazines," Megan said again, "or homework. What's it going to be?"

"Um, magazines," I said, trying to sound normal. "I'm caught up in social studies."

I'd done all my homework while waiting up for Mom to get home from work the night before. When she came in, she muttered a quick "It's late; get to bed" in my direction before heading down the hall.

This morning? No better. She'd puttered around in her bedroom "getting ready" until we'd left for school. I'd tried to talk Caitlyn into busting in there with me and confronting her, but as usual, my sister didn't want to make waves. So instead we'd sat in the kitchen, just the two of us, eating our cereal and wondering what exactly to do about the situation.

At least that was what *I* was wondering. Cait? Who knew?

Soon Megan and I were ensconced at a little round table in the corner, the latest issues of *Vogue*, *Seventeen*, and various other fashion mags spread out in front of us. Well, the latest issues available in the sleepy little Aura Middle School library, anyway. Which meant most of them were about six months old.

Normally that would have annoyed me. Today? I barely noticed. I sat there flipping past pictures of models and makeup and who knew what else, still focused on my problems.

After a while, I became vaguely aware that Megan was talking to me. Mostly because she started poking me in the arm. Hard.

"Ow." I pushed her hand away. "What?"

"Have you heard a single word I've said in the past ten minutes?" she demanded, looking peeved.

I bit back a sarcastic response. "Sorry," I said

instead. "Guess I'm a little distracted today."

"Oh." Her expression immediately switched from annoyed to worried. "Everything okay?"

"Sure," I responded automatically.

"Really? You've been acting kind of—I don't know. Just not yourself. I noticed earlier, too."

I was touched that she seemed so concerned. Not sure what to say, I toyed with the key-shaped necklace, which I hadn't taken off since it had arrived.

Megan's gaze followed my hand. "Ooh, cool pendant!" she said. "Where'd you get it?"

I hesitated, wanting to tell her the truth. Maybe not the whole truth—I had no interest in spending my twelfth birthday in the loony bin. But that didn't mean I couldn't tell her the non-loony parts, right?

"Actually, it's a long story." I glanced around to make sure nobody was close enough to hear us. "But you have to swear not to tell anyone, okay? Like, not even Lav or the others."

"Cross my heart," she said, tracing a manicured finger in a big X across the front of her cute pastel-striped shirt.

I took a deep breath. "It's about my—my dad."

"Your dad?" Megan looked confused.

"He died when I was a baby," I said. "I don't remember him at all."

She leaned forward, looking stricken. "Oh, Cass! I had no idea. I'm sorry."

"Thanks." I shrugged. "The thing is, my mom is really weird about him. She won't tell us anything, and Cait and I have always wanted to know more."

"Of course you do!" She nodded emphatically. "You must be dying of curiosity. Why won't she talk about him?"

"I don't know. And I can't really even ask." I grimaced, picking at a peeling bit of paint on the edge of the table. "If you knew my mom, you'd know she gets mad if you ask too many questions. And trust me, you don't want to get her mad if you can help it."

"Oh." Megan looked thoughtful for a second. "Do you have any other relatives you could ask?"

"Not really." I shrugged. "I mean, I've got plenty of family on my mom's side. But they won't cross her. Plus I'm not sure how much any of them even know, since Mom got married when she was stationed overseas." I took a deep breath. "But actually, the reason I'm thinking about all this now is because our grandmother—my dad's mom—sent Cait and me a package with this necklace and a letter, too. It came yesterday. Until then, we didn't even know she existed."

"Really?" Megan exclaimed. "What'd the letter say?"

"Good question." I slumped in my seat. "Mom grabbed it before we could read more than, like, the first few lines."

"Whoa." Megan fell silent for a moment. "I don't know what to say. I mean, it's hard for me to imagine not knowing everything about my family." Her mouth twisted into a half smile. "Sometimes it feels like it's basically Aura's town history!"

I chuckled. "Yeah, I can see how that could be a problem, too."

She smiled. "So I don't know how much help I can be. But still, I'm here for you, Cassie, if you need to talk or whatever."

"Thanks." Megan was being so cool that I was half tempted to share the rest of my family secret.

But only half. She might be understanding, but it was asking a lot to expect her to believe I could predict the future. I hardly believed it myself.

So instead, I grabbed her hand and squeezed it. But as soon as I touched her, my vision went all fuzzy, and Megan's sympathetic face faded into the background.

Overlaid on top of it was a much brighter, more vivid Megan. But this Megan wasn't sitting in the library. She was pushing open a big wooden gate into a grassy yard dotted with trees, carrying a small bag with the logo of the Adams General Store stamped on it. An adorable little brown-and-white dog leaped up to greet her, almost knocking her over. Vision-Megan laughed, grabbing the dog and cuddling him before setting him down and hurrying off across the yard.

I gulped, wanting to break the connection. But for some reason, I couldn't move. It was as if I was locked into the vision, which was so bright it was practically blinding me.

Luckily the minions rushed over right then. One grabbed Megan's shoulder and kind of shook her. That jostled her hand out of mine, and I fell back, the vision blinking away.

"Oh my gosh, you guys," Emily exclaimed, looking frantic. "We are so dead!"

"Settle down, ladies," Megan said, rolling her eyes at the minions. "What's wrong?"

They started babbling about something, but I wasn't listening. I just sat there, taking deep breaths and feeling grateful that the other girls had interrupted at just the right moment. *Lucky*, I thought, touching my necklace again. Then again, I might not have needed luck if Mom hadn't snatched away the only thing that might help me make sense of all this.

I DIDN'T SEE Caitlyn until right before lunch. She looked startled when I grabbed her arm and yanked her out of the hallway and into an empty classroom.

"What are you doing?" she complained. "I want to get to the caf before they run out of dessert."

"I had a vision," I hissed, not really in the mood for small talk.

Her eyes widened. "You did? Who—when—what?"

"Megan." I quickly filled her in on the gist of what I'd seen.

By the time I finished, she was nodding. "Hey, that's great!" she exclaimed. "Don't you see what this means? I was right!"

I glared, not in the mood for cryptic optimism. "Right about what?"

"About how maybe it was just a coincidence that most of the stuff I was seeing was good and most of your stuff was—"

"Not good," I finished. Then I blinked. "Hey. You know, you have a point."

"I know, right?" She grinned. "I mean, what could be bad about Megan playing with an adorable puppy, right?"

"Yeah." For some reason, that made me feel a little better about having had another vision. "I just wish we still had that letter," I said with a frown.

"Because it sounded like our grandmother wanted to help us deal with this crazy Sight thing."

"I know, right?" Cait said. "It's one thing to randomly start having visions of the future. It's another thing to find out it runs in your family!"

I nodded. "Too bad we don't even know our grandmother's name. We have to get that letter back!"

"We can try." Caitlyn looked dubious. "Anyway, let's talk about it later. I'm starving."

"Okay." I followed her out of the room. She immediately spotted the dork patrol heading for the caf and rushed off to catch up to them.

I glanced around for my own friends. My gaze caught on Gabe Campbell leaning against the wall nearby. He was staring at me with narrowed eyes.

Uh-oh. Was he just hating on me in general, as usual? Or was there a chance he'd heard what Caitlyn and I were saying? He was awfully close to that classroom door . . .

I shook off the thought as I saw Megan and Lavender coming toward me. Good old Greasy Gabe didn't need a reason to look suspicious, right? And I had enough to worry about right now without adding him to the mix. I was just being paranoid.

"Guys!" I called to my friends, turning away from Gabe. "Over here!"

5
CAITLYN

"SO DID YOU decide what we're doing for your birthday?" Liam asked as we left the lunch line and wandered toward our table, where Bianca was saving us seats.

I shook my head. "Cassie and I haven't had much time to discuss it yet."

"Did you tell her about my monster-movie idea?" he asked eagerly.

Before I could answer, Gabe Campbell stomped past us. "Out of the way, freaks," he said, purposely bumping Liam hard with one shoulder. He paused just long enough to glare at me. "Especially *you*, superfreak!"

"Ow," Liam muttered, rubbing his arm as Gabe took off. "What was that all about?"

"Who knows?" I stared after Gabe. He was always calling me names—Cassie, too—but "super-freak" was a new one.

Bianca glanced up from her book as Liam and I sat down. "Hey, Caitlyn," she said. "Ms. Xavier was just here looking for you."

"She was?" I glanced around. "Why?"

"Don't know," Bianca replied. "But here she comes again."

Sure enough, the teacher was barreling toward us with a big smile on her face and her patchwork peasant skirt swishing around her legs. "Caitlyn!" she exclaimed breathlessly. "You rushed out of class so fast that I didn't get a chance to touch base with you. Have you given any thought to my idea?"

"Your idea?" I'd nearly forgotten our conversation the day before. "You mean about the project?"

"Yes, of course." She leaned on the table, almost putting her hand down on Bianca's sandwich. "I mentioned it to your twin, too, but she said she'd have to speak to you about it. So what do you say? Are you two in?"

Out of the corner of my eye, I could see my friends trading perplexed looks. "I've been so busy I haven't had a chance to think about it yet. Can I get back to you?"

"Of course. No pressure!" She laughed loudly, then patted me on the arm. "I just really think it could be . . . enlightening. Hmm? But yes, let me know what you decide after you've discussed it with Cassie."

"Okay."

"What was that all about?" Bianca asked once the teacher had gone.

I sighed. "Nothing. Just some idea she had about Cassie and me working together on the social studies project." I filled them in on what Ms. Xavier had said. "What's the deal with her, anyway?" I added. "She seems almost obsessed with the whole twin thing."

"She's interested in all kinds of weird stuff." Liam

shot me an apologetic look. "Not that being twins is weird."

"It's okay; I know what you mean." I smiled at him. "So what else is she into?"

He shrugged. "Lots of things. Like last year she decided everyone would learn more if she hung crystals all over the room. Oh, and she was into aromatherapy for a while. She made the whole school smell like lavender for months."

"The principal stopped her from teaching a unit on voodoo, though," Bianca put in. "That was too much for Aura."

"She's not from here," Liam added. "She married into Aura. Her husband's family has been here forever, but she lived in New Orleans before."

I was already losing interest in Ms. Xavier. Whatever her obsession with twins, it was a little odd, but no biggie. Kind of cute, actually.

"I'll have to let her down easy on the twin project idea," I said.

Liam took a sip of his water. "So you're not going to do it?"

"No way. It's been hard enough to get Cassie to work with me on our birthday party—doing a social studies project with her would be a disaster!" I laughed. "Anyway, speaking of the party, Cass and I are supposed to figure out a plan tomorrow." Suddenly I had a great idea. "Hey, why don't you both come over? You can help us brainstorm."

"Sure, that sounds fun," Liam agreed immediately.

"Cool! Bianca? What about you?" Neither of my friends had been to my house yet, and I was looking forward to hanging out with them more outside of school.

"Can I let you know in the morning?" Bianca said slowly. "I'm not sure if I can make it or not."

"Sure, no problem." I smiled at her, waiting for an explanation. But Bianca was staring down at her food, her brow furrowed. She looked sad again— like she had yesterday. I couldn't help feeling a flash of worry. What was going on with her?

"Liam! Dude!" A large boy with spiky brown hair rushed toward us. Right behind him was a smaller kid with lots of freckles and a crooked smile.

Liam grinned at them. "Josh, Goober," he said. "What's up?"

The three boys started jabbering about some science fiction movie they'd seen on TV, and Bianca added a few sarcastic comments, that brief sadness no longer evident on her face.

Like Mom says, don't borrow trouble, I told myself.

"LIGHTS OUT, GIRLS." Mom stuck her head into our room just long enough to flick the switch off.

"Good night," I said, but she was already gone.

Cassie and I were both in bed. I was reading a book, and she was lying on her side fiddling with the necklace from the package.

"Typical," she muttered. "Ever since yesterday, it's like Mom can't get away from us fast enough."

"Yeah." I sighed. "It's pretty obvious she doesn't want to talk about what happened."

"Understatement of the century," Cassie said with a snort. "But she can't avoid us forever." She sat up, staring at me in the dim light seeping through the window from the streetlamps. "But listen—I've been meaning to tell you. I saw Gabe Campbell today after we were talking. You know, before lunch?"

"Yeah? So?" I was only half listening, distracted by thoughts of Mom. Why had she taken our letter and that dusty old book? And why did she shut us down every time we tried to ask about it? I kept telling myself she had to have a reason. The trouble was, I couldn't for the life of me figure out what that reason might be.

"He was standing right outside the room," Cassie went on. "And he gave me a super-intense look when I passed him."

That got my attention. "I saw Gabe in the caf right after that, and he called me a superfreak." I gulped, as a reason for that particular name occurred to me. "What if he heard us?"

"I don't know. But it gives us even more reason to figure things out fast." Cassie sounded grim. "And now that we know there's someone out there who can help us, there's no reason to bumble along like idiots."

"You mean our grandmother?"

"Duh, of course." She was playing with the necklace again. "We have to get that letter back. No matter what."

"Okay." I felt a little uneasy. It was too dark to see Cassie's expression clearly, but she sounded pretty determined. "Maybe we should just try talking to Mom again. We could tell her about the visions and ask her to help."

"What's the point? She has to know we're having visions. Otherwise, why did she freak out when she saw that letter?"

I sat up. "Wait. Maybe it's not about the Sight at all, though. Maybe she just doesn't want us to find out anything about our dad."

"But why? It has to be connected." She tapped the pendant against her chin. "She's kept the truth about Dad's family from us all these years. We need to find out why."

I didn't say anything. Lying back down, I couldn't help wondering if my sister was right. It stressed me out to think that Mom would keep such an important secret from us. I was trying to assume she had a good reason, but . . .

"Anyway, we can't talk to her tomorrow," Cassie broke into my thoughts. "She's working all day, remember?"

"Right." Mom hadn't talked much at dinner this evening, but she'd told us that much. "Remind me to check with her in the morning—I forgot to tell her I invited Liam and Bianca over to help with our party plans."

"You did?" Cassie said. "Because I invited Megan and Lav. They're coming right after lunch. Megan even managed to get out of helping her mom with some dumb dinner to come. I'm sure they'll have lots of good ideas, so maybe you should call your friends and cancel."

"Why?" I felt a flash of annoyance. "Your friends aren't the only ones who can come up with something fun."

"I beg to differ." She let out a snort. "When I need to plan a nerd convention, I'll totally call Liam. For a cool birthday party? Not so much."

I frowned. "Whatever, Cassie," I said with a flash of irritation. Every time I thought maybe Cass and I were connecting for a change, she had to go and say something obnoxious. Something that reminded me just how different we'd become. "They're coming, okay? You and your *cool* friends will just have to deal."

"Whatever yourself," she retorted. Flopping back onto her bed, she pulled the sheet up to her chin. "Now be quiet so I can go to sleep."

6
CASSIE

"GEEZ, I THOUGHT she'd never leave," I muttered, flipping back the curtain in the front window.

I watched as Mom's car backed out of the driveway and tooled off down the road. Then I let the curtain fall.

Caitlyn was observing me from the sofa, where she'd spent the last few minutes flicking idly through the TV channels. "What are you going to do?" she asked, switching off the TV.

I glanced at her. We hadn't talked much that morning. Caitlyn seemed a little cranky. Was she seriously holding a grudge because I'd pointed out that her friends were nerds? I was just being honest.

But I couldn't focus on that. I had more important things to worry about, so I was doing my best to ignore her attitude.

"I'll tell you what I'm going to do." Striding across the room, I yanked open the drawer in Mom's desk, which was tucked into a corner of the living room. "I'm going to find that letter."

"What?" Cait sat up straighter, looking alarmed. "Hold on. We're not supposed to go in Mom's desk."

"Well, people aren't supposed to steal other people's mail either." I shoved aside some pens and a pair of scissors, digging into the back of the drawer. "Isn't that a federal offense or something? Mom could totally arrest herself for that."

Caitlyn jumped to her feet and came a few steps forward. "So talk to her about it," she said. "You can't just rip the house apart looking for that letter!"

"Can't I? Watch me." There was no sign of our stuff in the desk, so I headed for the hall. "It's got to be somewhere, right?"

"Cassie, stop." Cait followed as I headed toward Mom's bedroom. "Seriously. If Mom catches you, we're both dead!"

"She had no right." The more I thought about what Mom had done, the angrier I got. "That package was addressed to us. She shouldn't have taken it away. Especially with no explanation."

I shoved open the door. Mom's bedroom was as neat as a pin. Twenty years in the army and lots of moves had taught her to travel light. The only pieces of furniture in there other than the bed were a small table with a single drawer and a bureau with a mirror.

Stepping over to the bedside table, I yanked open the drawer. Caitlyn grabbed my arm.

"Cassie, stop!" she pleaded, on the verge of tears. "This isn't right. Mom's going to notice everything's messed up, and then she'll never trust us again."

That stopped me. Whirling around, I glared at

my sister. "That's fine," I spat out. "Because I'll never trust her again either!"

Cait's eyes widened with horror. "Don't say that."

"Why not?" Hands on hips, I glared at her. Even a Goody-Two-shoes like Cait had to see what was going on by now. "Think about it, Cait. She knew what was happening to us all along and didn't say a word."

"We don't know that for sure," she said.

"Sure we do." I returned my attention to the drawer. "It's the only explanation for how she knew to grab that letter when she saw it."

My sister was silent for a second, watching as I slammed the drawer shut and turned my attention to the bureau. "Maybe," she said at last. "I mean, I've been trying to think of another reason, but I haven't come up with one yet."

"That's because there isn't one." I opened the bottom bureau drawer and shoved aside a pile of shirts.

"Okay. But even if Mom knew about the Sight, she had no way of knowing we were actually having visions. Maybe she was waiting for us to say something. Maybe she assumed we'd tell her about something like that."

"Are you serious?" I couldn't believe she could be so dense. "Yeah, okay, maybe she didn't know right away. But what about what happened at the football game last week? If she didn't know before, she had to know then."

"Oh. I forgot about that." Caitlyn bit her lip. "Still . . ."

I didn't bother to respond as I dug through more of Mom's clothes. No matter how sunny-side up she could be, Caitlyn had to realize I was right. We'd both seen visions involving Gabe's uncle breaking into the police station to frame Mom, and because of them, we got to him before he did any serious damage. Oh, we hadn't come right out and told her what we'd seen. But I'd never forget that long, searching look she'd given us when we'd urged her to go check on things at the precinct *just in case.*

"I still don't think you should be doing this," Caitlyn said after a moment. "Two wrongs don't make a right."

I rolled my eyes, not bothering to respond. "Where'd she put that stupid thing, anyway?" I muttered, slamming the top drawer shut.

I headed for the closet. It was just as tidy as the rest of the room. There were only a few places to search—a couple of shoe boxes and garment bags.

As I slid a hand into the pockets of Mom's winter coat, I heard a noise and glanced back. Caitlyn was easing open the top drawer of the bureau.

"I already looked in there, genius," I told her.

"Duh," she said. "I was here. I watched you. I'm trying to neaten it up so Mom doesn't figure out what you did."

Despite my mood, I almost laughed. "You? Clean? Don't worry, I'm not planning to leave any evidence. I'll fix everything after I find the stuff."

But I didn't find it. There was no sign of the package, the letter, or the dusty old book. Not in Mom's closet; not anywhere in her bedroom. It wasn't in any of the other closets in the house either. I even checked the cabinets in the bathroom.

Finally I stomped into the living room, glancing

around for more hiding places. "Where could it be?" I exclaimed.

Caitlyn was still following me around. "Think about it, Cassie," she said with a hint of sarcasm. "Mom took everything with her when she left for work the other day. Which means it's probably at the police station. Are you planning to rip that apart next?"

I stared at her, my heart sinking. "You're right," I said. "It probably is at work. Or maybe in her car—I can try to check there later."

She frowned. "Are you going to chill out now? Because my friends will be here soon, and I'd rather not have them see you acting like a maniac."

Once again, she was right. Checking my watch, I realized that Megan and Lavender would be arriving in a few minutes. "I'm done," I said. "At least for now. But that doesn't mean I'm giving up."

Cait didn't respond. I shrugged, then headed back into Mom's room to straighten up her drawers.

By the time I emerged, Liam and Bianca were there, lounging on the sofa, and Caitlyn was puttering around in the kitchen.

"Hi, Cassie," Liam said. "Happy almost birth-day."

"Thanks," I muttered, heading to the kitchen to grab a glass of water. Playing detective was thirsty work, especially during a heat wave in a house with inadequate AC.

"Want some lemonade?" Caitlyn asked. "I made it earlier."

"No thanks." I gulped down half my water. "So where are you and your friends planning to hang out? Because the girls will be here any second."

"What do you mean? We're planning to stay right where we are." She glanced out through the archway into the living room.

"Then where are my friends and I supposed to go?" I demanded.

Before she could say anything, there was a knock on the door. I hurried over to answer.

"Hey, Cassie," Megan said with a smile as she and Lavender stepped inside. "Cute house."

"Thanks." Megan seemed sincere, but I couldn't miss the look of disdain on Lav's face as she glanced around the small living room. I couldn't help seeing it through her eyes. The dingy way-off-white carpet. The cloudy glass in the windows. The missing trim around one of the doorways. I'd already known the place was a dump. Somehow, though, all the work Mom made us do when we first moved in had disguised that a little. But only a little.

Finally Lavender's gaze settled on Liam and Bianca. "What are *they* doing here?" she said.

"Sorry," I murmured. "My sister invited them."

"Does that mean they'll be at your party?" Lavender sounded surprised.

"Sssh," Megan hushed her. "It's no big deal. The more the merrier." She waved and smiled brightly at the pair. "Hi, guys! What's up?"

Bianca just blinked, surprised that Megan was talking to her. No wonder. It was probably the first time ever.

"Come on over here," I told my friends, leading the way toward the dining table. "Want some snacks or something?"

"No thanks." Lavender settled herself in Mom's

chair. "We stopped at the store on the way over to drop off Amigo with my cousin."

"Amigo?" Liam echoed curiously.

"My dog," Lavender said, actually flashing him a brief smile. "He hates staying home alone, and he loves greeting all the customers. Everyone loves him, too—I swear the store sells, like, ten times as much stuff when he's there." She giggled, then glanced at me. "Anyway, while we were there we had some ice cream."

Thanks for bringing some for me, I thought.

Lavender's family had been in Aura almost as long as Megan's. They owned the town's general store and often gave free snacks to Lav and her friends when they stopped in.

A second later Caitlyn came in and passed out lemonade and cookies to Liam and Bianca. "Okay," she said, sitting down cross-legged on the carpet in front of the sofa. "Let's talk about this party."

"Sure!" Liam replied eagerly. "I have lots of ideas. My favorite is a monster-movie theme. We'd dress up as our favorite monsters, and . . ."

"Monsters?" Lavender let out a loud snort. "Absolutely not."

"Oh." Liam looked momentarily deflated. Then he brightened. "Okay, then how about an outer space theme? I did that for my ninth birthday, and it was really fun."

Megan looked dismayed. "Um . . . ," she began.

"No way," Lavender said bluntly. "Look, Cassie. You need to have a real party—no stupid themes, no monsters or space aliens." She glared at Liam, then glanced around the room. "But now that I'm here, this place is definitely way too small. Have you checked into the hotel option?"

"Hotel option?" Caitlyn echoed. "What are you talking about?"

"There's a really nice hotel in Six Oaks," Megan explained. "Lots of people throw parties in their ballroom."

"Sounds nice," Cait said. "But also expensive."

"I'm sure it's not that bad." Lav shrugged. "Anyway, you only turn twelve once, right?"

"Didn't you hear her?" Bianca spoke up. "She

said it's too expensive. And it's their party, not yours."

Lavender's head whipped around to stare. That was probably the most I'd ever heard from Bianca.

"Excuse me?" Lavender exclaimed. "You don't have to be rude!"

"Apparently I do," Bianca shot back. "Because you're not listening to anything anyone says."

"Guys, guys," Caitlyn said soothingly. "Let's not fight, okay?"

Easy for her to say—her friend had started it! But going off on my sister wouldn't help. Instead I touched the key necklace, which for some reason I found oddly comforting.

"Caitlyn's right," Megan spoke up. "Let's just talk about the party, okay?"

"That's what I was trying to do." Lavender glared at Bianca. "Until *she* got all in my face."

Liam blinked. "No, she didn't," he said. "She just said—"

"I heard what she said," Lavender cut him off. "Unfortunately."

Bianca didn't respond. She wasn't really looking at anyone.

"Sorry, Cait," she said softly, standing up. "Could I use your bathroom?"

"Sure," Cait said. "Down the hall, first door on the right."

Bianca nodded and headed that way. As she passed me, her arm brushed mine.

I gasped as a vision hit me hard and fast. It was Bianca, of course. Her face was so clear that it was impossible to miss how upset she looked as she rushed past a sign that read SIX OAKS HOSPITAL: ENTRANCE.

7
CAITLYN

I WATCHED BIANCA disappear down the hall, a little worried. What had that outburst been about? It seemed out of character for her to fight with anyone—even Lavender Adams at her most annoying.

Then again, I hadn't known Bianca very long. I glanced at Liam. He didn't look particularly worried, which made me relax a little.

I tensed up again as Cassie rushed over to me. "I need to talk to you in private," she hissed. "Now."

TWINTUITION: DOUBLE TROUBLE

"Huh?" I blurted out.

She dragged me toward the back hallway. "We'll be right back," she called to the others.

"Yeah," I added. "Right back." I could only hope Lavender and Megan wouldn't team up and kick Liam out of the house before I returned.

Cassie pulled me past our bedroom and out the door leading onto the tiny back deck. The sun was glaring down without a cloud to be seen, and I felt myself start to sweat instantly.

"What is it?" I demanded. "It's boiling out here."

She finally let go of my arm and turned to face me. "I just had a vision," she said. "About Bianca."

"What? When?"

"Just now, when she bumped into me on her way past." She told me what she'd seen.

"The hospital?" I exclaimed. "Did it look like she was hurt?"

"No, just really freaked out." Cassie shrugged. "Maybe like someone else was hurt. Or . . ." She gulped. "Maybe even worse. I mean, she looked *really* upset."

"Wow." I thought about that for a second. "Do you think we should—"

At that moment Lavender burst out onto the deck. "Would you two get back in here?" she complained. "Because Liam seems to actually think you'd consider having all your guests come dressed as cavemen."

"We'll deal with it," Cassie told her.

Lavender nodded. Her hazel eyes swept the tiny backyard. So far Mom had focused most of her attention on the front of the house. All she'd done back here was mow the patchy grass and trim the overgrown hedges that divided it from the neighbors on either side. I'm sure Lavender thought it looked kind of shabby. Not that I cared what she thought.

"Good thing it's too hot for an outdoor party," she said at last. Suddenly her eyes widened. "Wait, I'm a genius!" she exclaimed.

Cassie smiled faintly. "Okay," she said. "Why?"

Lavender grabbed her arm, looking excited. "Pool party!" she blurted out. "It's perfect! You can have it at Megan's house, and it won't cost you a penny!"

"Wha—" I began.

Too late. Lavender whirled and raced back into the house, shouting Megan's name.

"Come on," Cassie said. We followed her inside.

By the time we reached the living room, Lavender was dancing around in front of Megan. ". . . and I heard the weather's supposed to stay hot through next weekend," she was saying. "So it's perfect, right? What do you think?"

"Hold on," I began.

Megan was already nodding. "Sure," she said with a smile. She glanced at Cassie, then at me. "It would be superfun to have your birthday at my pool. I'm sure my parents will say yes."

"Text them right now." Lavender grabbed Megan's purse, digging into it for her phone. "Go on!"

"Wait!" I could feel the situation spiraling out of control. I glanced at Bianca, who had returned from the bathroom, and at Liam. As it was, my friends were being treated like losers right here in my own house. How much worse would it be at Megan March's place? Besides, Megan wasn't even my friend. I wouldn't only be in danger of feeling like a guest at my own party, I'd risk feeling like an *unwanted* guest!

But Liam was smiling. "Pool party?" he said. "Awesome! That's even better than my caveman idea."

He actually looked excited. I stared at him in surprise, distracted enough that by the time I returned my attention to Megan, she'd sent her text.

"There, I just asked," she said. "It's really only a formality, though. They'll say yes. My parents love throwing parties."

"True story," Lavender agreed. "The Hawaiian luau they threw last summer to raise money for the Six Oaks Hospital? Absolutely epic."

Her mention of the hospital reminded me of Cassie's vision. I glanced over and found her staring at me. We'd discovered that we could sometimes change the future by figuring out what was happening in our visions. That meant there was a chance of helping Bianca avoid the terrible scene Cass had just observed. But only if we could figure out what was going to happen in time to stop it.

I wandered over to the sofa. "Hey, guys, make room," I said lightly, squeezing in between Bianca and Liam. I leaned closer to Bianca, making sure our shoulders touched. If I got a vision about her, too, maybe it would give us more information.

But I got nothing. That was another thing Cassie and I had discovered—it wasn't that easy to bring on a vision. They seemed to come whenever they felt like it.

I tuned back to the rest of the room. Cassie, Megan, and Lavender were chattering about food and decorations and invitations. Liam was listening with interest.

"We don't have much time," Megan said, "if we're throwing this party a week from today."

Cass nodded. "I've got a good design program on my laptop," she said. "I'll start working up an invitation. That way I can e-mail it to everyone as soon as Megan's parents give the official okay."

"Wait," I said. "Aren't we going to talk about the other ideas we all had?"

"What's the point? The pool party is perfect."

Lavender checked her watch. "Come on, Megs. Let's go back to my store. We can get some of the stuff we need there, then take Amigo to the park while Cassie works on the invitation."

Bianca stood up as soon as the two girls left. "I should go, too," she said softly. "I have, um, stuff to do at home."

"I'll walk you," Liam offered. He tossed me a sloppy salute. "Thanks for the lemonade, Caitlyn. I can't wait for the party!"

Soon they were gone, too. Cassie was at the dining table, already leaning over her laptop. I stomped over and glared down at her.

"What was that all about?" I demanded.

She blinked up at me. "What?"

"You know what." I crossed my arms. "You and your friends totally took over! It's supposed to be my party, too. Don't I even get a vote?"

She shrugged. "So why didn't you say something?"

"I tried!" I exclaimed. "The trouble is, Lavender never listens to anyone but herself. And maybe her dog."

I noticed Cassie touching the key-shaped necklace that had come in the package. She'd been wearing it nonstop since it had arrived.

"And, by the way, that's supposed to be for both of us, too." I pointed at the pendant. "I haven't even had a chance to touch it yet. Hand it over."

Cassie frowned, and for a second I thought she might refuse. Then she pulled the necklace off over her head.

"Whatever," she said, tossing it at me. "Be my guest. Just try not to lose it, okay? You're not exactly famous for keeping your stuff neat."

Ignoring that, I checked out the pendant. It really was pretty cool. There was an etching of a tree on the top part, and little scratches and dents in the metal that made it look really old. I slipped it on over my head, and the pendant settled against my skin, feeling oddly warm.

When I glanced at my sister, she was watching me with narrowed eyes. Then she turned back to her computer.

"Let me know who else you want to invite to the party besides the king and queen of the dweebs," she said as her fingers flew over the keyboard. "I need to send this out soon."

BY THE NEXT morning, my annoyance had worn off. Most of it, anyway. I was still peeved that Cass and her friends were railroading me into this pool party. But it was too late to worry about that now. The vision about Bianca, on the other hand, might still be fixable. My sister and I needed to get over our petty disagreements and figure out what to do.

Cassie had already left the room by the time I woke up, so I pulled on some clothes and went looking for her. She was eating breakfast while Mom puttered around in the kitchen.

"Oh, Caitlyn, you're up," Mom said when I entered. "Good. I was about to come wake you. I don't have to be at work until tonight, so how about a trip to the mall—the three of us?"

Cassie looked up in surprise. "The mall?"

Mom nodded. "You keep telling me about all the shopping you've been doing there," she said with a smile. "Reckon I should see for myself."

I stared at her. She was acting as if nothing had happened. That wasn't like her. Mom believed in confronting issues, not avoiding them. Well, except when those issues had anything to do with our father.

"You want to go to the mall? Really?" Cassie sounded suspicious.

Mom chuckled. "Yes, really. I've been so busy with the move and the new job that I haven't had a moment to buy you two birthday gifts yet." She shrugged. "This way you can pick out what you want and save yourself a trip back to exchange everything."

"Sure, Mom," I said uncertainly. "That sounds fun."

Cass shoveled the last bit of cereal into her mouth. "Yeah, I'm always up for the mall," she said. "Just give me a minute to get dressed."

"Meet you at the car in ten minutes," Mom said,

hurrying toward her room.

That left me alone in the kitchen. Once again, I apparently didn't get a vote.

"Guess we're going to the mall," I muttered with a sigh.

8

CASSIE

THE SIX OAKS Galleria was pretty pathetic compared to the shopping in San Antonio. But it was miles better than the collection of dusty old stores in archaic Aura. It felt kind of weird to be there with my family, though. Mom hated malls, and Caitlyn had the fashion sense of a gnat. If not for my helpful advice, she'd probably go to school in sweats and sneakers every day.

I eyed Mom as we pushed our way through the

heavy glass doors. Cold air hit us—they had the AC cranked up to arctic in there. It felt good after the swampy weather outside, even though I sort of wished I'd brought a sweater. The mall was packed, which wasn't surprising. What else was there to do on a boring Sunday in the middle of nowhere?

"What do you say, girls?" Mom said cheerfully, glancing around. "Where should we go first?"

That was weird. Mom never sounded happy about shopping. Especially if she had to deal with crowds to do it.

"Why don't we start with the party shop?" I suggested, squinting in the direction of the directory as I tried to remember where I'd seen the store. I'd never been inside—streamers and balloons hadn't been on the shopping list when I was there with my friends—but I vaguely recalled the place looking pretty well stocked.

"Party shop?" Mom echoed. "Is that the name of the latest teen clothing store?"

"No, I mean an actual party store," I said, heading

in the direction I thought the place might be. "We'll need some decorations for next weekend."

"Party?" Mom's voice went sharp. "What party?"

"You didn't tell Mom about the party?" Caitlyn asked. "Because I didn't either."

Oops. Now that she mentioned it . . . "Our birthday party," I said, barely managing to avoid adding a *duh* at the end. Knowing Mom, that wouldn't go over well, and I didn't want to have to buy all the party stuff out of my allowance money. I was saving up for a cute pair of jeans I had seen. "We meant to tell you—Megan's parents offered to let us have it at their house. They have a pool."

Mom stopped short, causing the teenage couple walking behind us to veer around us. The guy shot us a dirty look and a muttered curse, which Mom ignored.

"Hold on," she said, looking from me to Cait and back again. "I thought we agreed there wouldn't be a party this year."

"No, we didn't," I said. "We definitely didn't agree. You said we'd talk about it later."

Just one more subject we were supposed to talk about later, I thought. But once again, I opted not to mention that part out loud.

She frowned. "Look, I told you we could still do something special. How would you like to drive back to San Antonio for the day, have dinner at that Italian place you like so much?"

"No way." I shook my head. "This is our birthday we're talking about! We want a party."

I glanced at my sister, wondering if she was going to back me up. Judging by the look on her face, that would be a big fat no.

"I do love that Italian place," she said softly.

"Are you kidding me?" I exclaimed, glaring at her. Then I turned back to Mom. "You can't do this! I mean, it's a miracle I actually managed to find some cool friends in this ridiculous little middle-of-nowhere town. And now you want to make me look like a loser by forcing me to cancel the party? Are you seriously trying to sabotage me like that?"

Mom put her hands on her hips. "Cassandra," she said in a dangerous tone I'd never heard before, way beyond scarymama. "I don't appreciate——"

"Hey!" a loud voice interrupted. "Waters family!"

I spun around. Of all people, greasy Gabe Campbell was walking toward us. Right behind him was a teenage guy I didn't recognize, but with their matching smirks, I assumed they were related.

Mom quickly rearranged her expression from acute fury to polite impatience. "Hello," she greeted the boys as they reached us. "It's Gabriel, yes?"

"Hi, Ms. Waters." Gabe grinned at her. "This is my cousin Thad."

"Yo," Cousin Thad said, still sneering at us.

"What a coincidence running into y'all here," Gabe said. "It's almost, you know, supernatural or something, right?"

"I suppose." Mom looked a little confused.

Supernatural? Caitlyn and I exchanged a panicked look, both remembering Gabe lurking in the hall the other day. Did this mean he really had overheard us? Did he know our secret?

Not that it mattered if he was about to spill it to Mom, since she obviously already knew.

"Well, we'd better move along," Gabe said. "Nice seeing y'all."

He and his cousin disappeared into the crowd. Mom turned her attention back to us.

"Now, where were we?" she said. "About this party . . ."

"Never mind that," I blurted out. "Are we ever going to talk about how you stole our package?"

Caitlyn's eyes widened. Mom's narrowed. "Cassandra!"

"No, I'm serious! It's pretty obvious you don't want us to know anything about our father's side of the family. Why are you so determined to keep us in the dark about them?"

Mom scowled. "That's quite enough, Cassie!"

I glanced at Caitlyn, expecting her to jump in and suggest we cool off, or change the subject to the weather, or whatever other crazy thing Miss Always-Sunny-Inside-My-Head might come up with to keep the peace.

She didn't notice me, though, because she was staring at Mom. "Are you ever going to tell us about our dad?" she asked, half-cautious and half-plaintive. "Why don't you want us to know anything about him?"

Mom opened her mouth, then shut it again. She blinked at us, looking as if she'd suddenly developed severe indigestion. "It's not that—" she began. "I mean, the thing is . . ." She shook her head, her expression darkening. "Look, this isn't the time or the place. End of discussion."

"No way!" I yelled, so loudly that several shoppers turned to stare at us curiously. Lowering my voice, I met Mom's steely gaze with my own. "It's not right," I said, trying not to let my voice shake. "He's our *father*. We deserve to know. And that package came for us. Not you. It's ours, and you should give it back."

"Sorry," Mom retorted, not sounding sorry at all, "but that's impossible."

"No, it's not," I exclaimed. "We're not babies anymore—we're almost twelve, and—"

"No, I mean it's really not possible," Mom interrupted. "I already sent it back."

My jaw dropped. "Huh?"

"You what?" Caitlyn sounded confused.

"I sent it back," Mom repeated, emphasizing each word. "Return to sender."

My mind swirled. Was she serious? I could feel tears forming in my eyes.

Mom must have noticed, because her expression softened slightly. "Enough about that," she said briskly. "But maybe I was too hasty about the party. I'll have to speak to Megan's parents, of course. But I suppose a party would be a nice way for you two to settle in."

She didn't sound very sure of that. But I blinked back my tears, trying to see the silver lining here. Mom was still refusing to talk about our dad, and she'd sent our package back—the only thing that might have explained what was happening to us. But at least she wasn't going to insist on making me a social outcast.

At least there was that.

"OKAY, SO WAS that the least fun trip to the mall ever, or what?" I commented, flopping onto my bed.

It was late that evening. Mom had just left for her night shift at the precinct, ordering me and Cait to be in bed by ten. But I felt restless and wide-awake.

Caitlyn's only response was a grunt. She kept her eyes trained on her laptop, which was open on the bed in front of her.

We hadn't talked much since the mall debacle. Okay, we hadn't talked at all. Unless you counted "Pass the salt" at dinner.

What was she mad at me about now? Whatever it was, she needed to get over it. And not only because we had a party to plan. I could do that by myself.

What I couldn't do on my own was figure out the rest of the mess that was our lives. How could Mom have mailed back that package? And if the package was really gone, how were we ever going to find out more about this Sight thing? It was pretty obvious that Mom wasn't going to be any help at all. Pretty much the opposite, actually.

"Cait?" I said. "Earth to Cait."

She shot me a brief, annoyed look. "What? I have

to finish these word problems for tomorrow."

Her tone was anything but friendly. Fine. I wasn't going to beg her to talk to me. Clicking off the light on my bedside table, I turned my face to the wall and waited for sleep.

9
CAITLYN

I SAT IN homeroom on Monday feeling out of sorts. The B Boys were horsing around in the back of the room, playing keepaway with Biff's math book. They were making tons of noise, and it was giving me a headache.

But I knew it wasn't really the B Boys who were bugging me. I hated fighting with Cassie. I hated it a whole lot. And I could tell she'd wanted to make up the night before.

But I hadn't been ready then. Not because her

friends had hijacked the party. Whatever, I could deal with that. Not even because she kept calling Liam and Bianca nerds. I was used to that sort of thing from her.

That scene at the mall, though? That had shaken me up. For real. When Cassie had started going at Mom, it was like she'd totally forgotten they were in public. What was she expecting to happen, anyway? Mom didn't deal well with threats or tantrums, and she could be just as stubborn as Cassie. Confronting her like that? Not only was it guaranteed not to work, but it might even make her *less* likely to tell us the truth.

We needed Mom on our side right now if we ever wanted to figure out what was happening to us, and Cassie may have ruined that for us forever.

"I got my pool party invitation!" Liam said, breaking into my thoughts. "If you need an RSVP, consider this mine—I'll be there."

"Cool." I forced a smile, then glanced at Bianca. As usual, she was reading a book at her desk, her dark hair falling forward to block her face from view.

"What about you, Bianca? Did you get your invite?" I knew Cassie had e-mailed the whole guest list the night before. At least she'd said she had. I was actually a little surprised that she hadn't "forgotten" to send anything to my friends.

Bianca looked up briefly. "Yes, I got it," she said. "Thanks."

"Good." I waited for her to say she was coming, but she'd already gone back to her book.

"I just hope it stays nice and hot until then." Liam leaned back in his chair and smiled. "I haven't been to Megan's pool since third grade, but it's awesome!"

I was a little surprised he'd been to Megan's pool at all. The two of them weren't exactly bosom buddies, as far as I could tell.

"Third grade?" I echoed.

He nodded so vigorously his hair flopped over his eyes. "She had the whole class over for an end-of-the-year party," he explained. "It was supergreat!"

It was nice that he was so excited about the party. I just hoped it was as much fun as he was expecting. With Lavender in charge—or at least trying to be—I wasn't feeling too confident about that myself.

I glanced toward Lavender's seat. She wasn't there yet, but I couldn't help noticing someone else staring at me.

Gabe. He was leaning forward in his seat a couple of rows back, his eyes trained right on me. As usual he looked unfriendly, but this time there was a twinge of something else—an expression I couldn't quite read.

With a gulp, I turned away quickly. Had he been listening? I felt a flash of guilt. He hadn't exactly been nice to me and Cassie since we'd arrived in town. Still, it couldn't be fun hearing about a party you weren't invited to, and that made me feel bad.

At least until I remembered the last time he'd eavesdropped. Was that weird expression him feeling left out because of the party—or was he thinking about what he'd overheard the other day?

I touched the key-shaped necklace, which I'd been wearing since Saturday. Bianca looked up just in time to notice.

"Hey, neat necklace," she said. "Where'd you get it?"

"Thanks," I said. "It's, um, a family hand-me-down."

"I'm not surprised—it looks really old. Can I see?" She reached for the pendant.

As she touched it, her fingers brushed my skin. I froze as a strong vision hit me—of Bianca sitting in a bland beige chair, sobbing her eyes out!

I pulled back with a gasp. Luckily at that very second Liam managed to knock all his books off his desk. "Oops!" he said with a laugh.

Bianca turned to help him. As the two of them gathered up Liam's stuff, I sat there trying to get control of myself. Wow, that had been close. The vision had been so strong that there was no way it hadn't showed on my face. It was a coincidence that Bianca had been staring at the necklace instead of at me. And that Liam's clumsiness had distracted her at just the right moment.

The scene had been much brighter and clearer than any earlier visions. Even in that split second,

I'd seen people in scrubs wandering around, and a sign about visiting hours.

A hospital waiting room, I thought. That's where she'd been—or rather, where she was going to be.

Thinking about that made me go hot and cold all over. Whatever Bianca was doing in that waiting room, it was making her cry in public—something I could hardly imagine calm, quiet Bianca doing at all. So what was going on? I'd thought I was supposed to see only *good* things, and that vision was anything but good.

Did this mean our visions were changing? I'd hardly thought about it when I'd assured Cassie that she might be seeing good things as well as bad ones. Now I realized what else that meant—that I could see bad stuff as well as good. Yikes!

But more important, what had Bianca been doing at the hospital?

I glimpsed over at her. As I did, I noticed a slight movement behind me. Glancing back, I saw that Gabe had just leaned forward again. He was watching me with a curious little gleam in his eye. I forced a shaky smile, but he just raised an eyebrow and then turned away.

CASSIE DIDN'T WAIT for me after school, leaving me to walk home alone. When I entered the house, she was on the sofa flipping through a magazine.

"Hi," I said tentatively. "Is Mom home?"

"Nope," she replied without looking up. "She's working this afternoon. She told us at breakfast."

I nodded. Breakfast had been a brief, mostly silent meal, but now that she mentioned it, I did recall Mom going over her work schedule for the week.

"Listen, Cassie," I said. "I'm sorry I was short with you last night. Can we stop fighting already? Please?"

She finally looked at me and shrugged. "Yeah, that would be good. I'm sorry, too. You know, for letting my friends take over the party or whatever. I promise you can help us plan it and stuff. I also promise that everyone will have a great time, including your dor—uh, your friends." She grinned. "Even if I have to tie Lav's mouth shut to make it happen."

I smiled with relief. She seemed clueless about

why I'd been so annoyed with her yesterday, but at least she'd apologized for the other stuff. And yesterday suddenly didn't seem so important.

"Good," I said. "Let's both agree to stop getting mad over stupid stuff, okay? Because we really need to work together right now. On a lot of stuff."

"Sing it, sister." She tossed her magazine aside and stretched. "Can you believe Mom sent our package back?"

She had a point, but I didn't want to get sidetracked by another rant about Mom right now. "Wait, I have a question," I said quickly. "What exactly did you see in that vision the other day? The one about Bianca."

"Not much," she said. "It was pretty short. All I saw was her rushing past the hospital sign, heading for the door."

"And she looked upset?"

"Very." She nodded. "Like she was totally freaked out, actually."

"Oh." I sank onto the sofa next to her. "Because I had a vision about Bianca and the hospital today, too." I described what I'd seen.

"Wow," she said. "Obviously someone she knows is going to end up in the hospital, right?"

"Seems like it." I bit my lip. "And it's got to be someone she cares about a lot for her to be that upset. So what are we going to do about it?"

"You mean you want to try to change it? Stop it from happening?"

"Of course!" I said. "What if it's some kind of accident or something? That's totally the kind of thing we could stop, right?"

"I guess." She didn't sound too convinced.

"We have to try," I told her firmly. "Especially since I'm afraid whatever it is might happen soon."

"Why do you think that?"

"Because my vision was superstrong this time."

Cassie tilted her head. "Wait," she said. "It doesn't work that way, does it? I mean, my visions have been getting stronger all along, but it's been kind of gradual. At least until recently."

"Me, too," I agreed. "But this Bianca one was extra vivid."

"Mine was, too." She was chewing her lower lip now, the way she always did when she was thinking hard. "So was the one I had about Megan and the dog, though. And that was days ago already."

"How do you know that one hasn't happened yet, though?" I said. "It just showed Megan at home playing with a dog, right? There's no reason you'd even know when something like that happened. It could have come true the same day you saw it."

"I guess."

"And the last vision I had before this one was the one with Mom and that man," I went on. "It wasn't nearly as vivid as the Bianca one. And I know it's not going to happen anytime soon since I saw Christmas decorations." I smiled, pleased with my own logic. Maybe we'd figure out this Sight thing yet!

"I guess. Only we've never noticed a difference like that before." Cassie's eyes shifted down from my face, then suddenly went sharp and thoughtful. "Wait, were you wearing the necklace today? When you had your Bianca vision?"

"Yeah." I touched the pendant. Then I gasped.

"Oh my gosh! Were you wearing it when you had your stronger visions, too?"

Cassie nodded. "And it came from our grandmother," she said. "Maybe it's some kind of amulet or talisman." She blinked. "What's the difference between those, anyway?"

"Never mind that." I was pondering her theory. It definitely made sense—at least as much sense as any of this did. "I bet you're right. The pendant might be adding extra power to our visions or something like that." I shuddered and pulled it over my head. "If you're right, I don't think I want to wear it. My visions are strong enough without any help."

"Same here. We can hide it in my jewelry box— Mom never looks in there." Cassie grabbed the necklace. "But this is good news, right? It means we might have more time than you thought to figure out how to help Bianca."

"Yeah." I shuddered again, flashing back to my vision. "I hope so."

10
CASSIE

ON TUESDAY AT lunch, I couldn't help glancing across the caf at Caitlyn's table every five seconds or so. As usual, she was sitting with Liam and Bianca. Liam and Cait were chatting, while Bianca had her face buried in a book. No wonder the girl was so skinny—she seemed to care more about reading than anything else, even eating.

Not that I blamed her. It was chicken potpie day. Totally gross.

"Cassie? What do you think?" Lavender's sharp

voice broke into my thoughts. "Are you even listening?"

I blinked at her. "Sorry, what?"

Lav looked impatient. "I said, should we try to find a band to play at your party? My uncle's a musician—he might know someone."

"I still think a DJ is better," minion Emily said. "That way we can request our favorite songs and stuff."

"Both sound cool to me," Megan put in. "Or we could just do a playlist on one of our phones or something—then we could pick exactly what we want to hear. What do you think, Cass?"

"Oh." I shrugged. "I don't know. Isn't it going to be hard to find a band this close to the party?"

Megan and the others nodded. "DJ it is," minion Abby said, looking happy.

"Or playlist," minion Emily put in.

Lavender leaned across the table. "What's with you today, Cassie? It's like you're not even interested in planning your own party." She grabbed my shoulders and shook me. "Snap out of it already!"

I didn't answer. I couldn't. Because as soon as her hand touched me, I was plunged into another vision.

Real Lavender faded away. Overlaid on top of her was a brighter version of Lavender, this one dressed in a cute polka-dotted two-piece swimsuit. There was a gorgeous pool in the background; I was pretty sure I saw a slide and a waterfall and some really nice deck chairs, though the details were a little hard to see.

Then I saw Lavender's face, which was streaked with tears. She was sobbing, collapsed against Abby, who was hugging her while Emily patted her back. Behind them, I could barely see Megan standing a few feet away. She was crying, too, standing there with her arms wrapped around herself.

Then Lavender let go of me and flopped back into her seat. I grabbed a napkin and pretended to wipe my mouth, hoping nobody had noticed me spacing out for a second.

"Funny, Cass," Lav said, rolling her eyes. "Fine, if you want to play zombie like that, maybe I'll keep my ideas to myself from now on." She popped a carrot stick into her mouth, looking sulky.

"Relax, Lav," Megan said. "Cassie was just kidding around. Right, Cass?"

"Totally." I tried to smile and look normal, relieved that Megan had taken my vision space-out for goofing off. "I'm sorry, Lav. Your plans all sound great. I really appreciate the way you're helping make this party happen."

"Okay." Lavender sounded mollified, at least a little. "Then let's talk about food . . ."

They were off and running again, blabbing on about party details. I tried to pay attention, but it wasn't easy. Because now that I'd recovered from the surprise of the vision, I'd realized a couple of things.

For one, it seemed our theory was right. I wasn't wearing the necklace that day, and the vision hadn't been as supercharged as the last two I'd had. It was clear enough to see what was happening, but the background hadn't glowed with energy like the others, and the colors hadn't been quite as crazy bright.

Still, I'd been able to see enough to guess where

the vision was taking place. Megan's pool. Which meant one thing.

Whatever they're all upset about, it must happen at our party! I thought with a chill of horror. *What if it has something to do with our visions about Bianca?*

My gaze wandered across the cafeteria again. Bianca had actually torn her gaze away from her book and was looking at Caitlyn with a small smile. Was something going to happen at the pool party? Something so terrible that it made even Lavender cry?

But what? Maybe something was going to happen to someone Bianca cared about. Like one of Bianca's best friends. One of whom happened to be my sister.

Yikes. What if Cait was the reason Bianca was at the hospital? I tried to banish the thought as soon as it came. Maybe it was Liam who got hurt at the party. Bianca would be upset about that, too, right?

But no—Lavender wouldn't cry if Liam got hurt. She might be sort of sad or worried—she was human, after all. But crying as if her heart was breaking, like

I'd just seen her do in my vision? No way. Not for Liam.

Would she cry like that for Caitlyn? I studied Lav's face as she talked to the others. She'd been much friendlier to me since this party came along, but did she consider me enough of a friend to cry like that if my sister got hurt?

I didn't know, but I wasn't sure I was willing to take the chance. Maybe Mom had been right all along. Maybe it would be better if we didn't have a party this year. It was starting to feel like more trouble than it was worth.

"Hey, ladies." Brayden's voice interrupted my churning thoughts. He'd appeared at our table without me even noticing. Which tells you how distracted I was.

"Hi, Brayden," Lavender cooed. "What's up?"

"Not much." He shoved his hands in the pockets of his jeans and grinned at me. "Just wanted to say thanks for the party invitation, Cassie. I'll be there for sure."

"Great," I said, feeling my face go hot.

"Yeah, the party's going to be superfab!" Abby burbled. "Lav is picking out the music, and there's going to be tons of food and stuff."

"Sounds fun," Brayden said, still smiling at me.

I smiled back, suddenly not so eager to cancel after all. Besides, my friends were so excited about this. How could I back out now? No, there had to be another way . . .

". . . SO YOU'RE SURE it was Megan's pool in the vision?" Caitlyn said.

I shoved a forkful of peas into my mouth. Mom was working late, and Cait and I were eating the dinner she'd left us to heat up.

"Pretty sure," I said. "I mean, what other pool would it be? It must have been our party I saw."

"You didn't actually see us there, though," Cait pointed out.

"Yeah. That's part of the problem." I speared another pea and stared at it. "I'm worried that one of us could be, you know, the victim." My eyes widened as another thought occurred to me. "Or maybe *both* of us are going to be victims!"

A chill ran down my spine as I realized that theory made a weird kind of sense. Neither of us had appeared in any of the visions. Maybe Bianca was crying over Cait, and Lavender was crying over me.

"What could possibly happen to both of us at the same time?" Caitlyn said.

I grimaced. "Car crash, maybe?" I said. "Or the pool heater could go crazy and electrocute us. Lots of stuff could happen."

"Ugh! Don't even say that." Cait put down her fork, looking worried. "Maybe we should cancel. It's not worth someone getting hurt."

"Yeah, especially me," I joked. Then I sighed. "But we can't cancel. What would we tell everyone? We'd look like total flakes."

"That's better than ending up in the hospital," Cait said. She was staring into space, twirling the ends of her hair between her fingers. She always did that when she was deep in thought.

"What?" I demanded. "What are you thinking about?"

"That letter," she said. "I know we didn't get to read much of it. But the part we did see said something about us learning to manage our powers."

"I know. Too bad we didn't get the details." I frowned at Mom's empty seat.

Caitlyn shrugged. "At least now we know it's possible to control this, at least somewhat, right? Plus we think that necklace strengthens the visions or whatever. Our grandmother must have known that. She probably sent it to help us."

I was starting to see what she was getting at. "So maybe we should try to figure it out on our own?" I guessed. "We don't have much time, though. It's already Tuesday, and the party's on Saturday."

"I know, I know. But listen, I was also thinking about what Ms. Xavier said."

I grimaced. The social studies teacher had been bugging me every chance she got about her stupid idea for me and Cait to work together. Fat chance. It was bad enough that Cait and I had some bizarre twin-power thing going. We didn't need to do a report on it for the weirdest teacher in school.

"Things are strange enough around here without getting her involved," I said, reaching for the salt.

"I'm not talking about getting her involved," Cait said. "I was just thinking how she mentioned doing twin experiments—you know, to see if we could read each other's minds or whatever?"

"Twintuition," I said with a half smile. "That's what we used to call it when we tried to guess each other's thoughts, remember?"

"I remember." Cait smiled back. "So maybe we should give it a try. Do some experimenting, see if we can control the visions more. That'll give us a better chance of figuring out exactly what we've been seeing—and how to stop it."

I took another bite of my food while I thought about it. "I guess it couldn't hurt to try."

We finished eating quickly and cleared the table. Then we sat down again, facing each other.

"Now what?" I said.

"I'm not sure." Cait grabbed both my hands. "Let's try to focus and see if that brings on a vision."

I nodded, squeezing her hands. Closing my eyes,

I thought about Caitlyn. Pictured her face, her goofy laugh, the whole deal.

Nothing happened. After a little while, I opened my eyes.

"This isn't working," I said. "Anyway, we've tried this before, remember? Touching someone and hoping for a vision doesn't bring on a vision. If it did, we'd be having them practically nonstop. They come totally at random and we have no say when or where or who as far as I can tell."

"Okay." Cait bit her lip. "But it can't hurt to experiment a little more. I mean, we really don't know how it works, exactly. Maybe we should try hugging. More touching, more vision, right?"

I rolled my eyes as she jumped to her feet. But I stood, letting her wrap her arms around me.

I hugged her back, pressing myself against her. She smelled good.

"Hey," I said suspiciously. "Did you steal my new jasmine shampoo?"

"Cassie!" She pulled back. "We need to focus."

I pushed her away. "What's the point? This

doesn't make sense. I mean, I've had visions about people when I barely brushed against them—like Bianca, for instance. Why would hugging make any difference?"

"I don't know." She brushed her hair out of her eyes, looking as frustrated as I felt. "I'm just trying stuff, you know?"

Suddenly I snapped my fingers. "Duh," I said. "I know something we can try."

Rushing to our room, I dug the talisman out of my jewelry box and brought it back to the living room.

"Oh, right," Caitlyn said when she saw it. "Good point."

I grabbed her hand again, so we were both holding the pendant. It pressed against both of our palms as we stared at each other.

"Nothing's—" Cait began. Then she gasped and her eyes went unfocused.

That was all I saw clearly. Because the real Caitlyn was fading, replaced by a supervivid, Technicolor Caitlyn. She was standing in our front yard facing a stern-looking elderly white woman with excellent posture. The woman was scowling and appeared to be yelling as Cait cowered.

The buzzing was so loud that my head felt ready to explode. With great effort, I pulled back.

The pendant fell to the floor, and the vision was gone.

"Whoa!" Cait gasped out. "I had one—did you?"

"Uh-huh." I told her what I'd seen.

"Weird," she said when I finished. "I saw an older woman in mine, too. Gray hair in a bun, thin and kind of tall?"

"That's the one," I said. "She was wearing a blue suit, I think."

"In mine, she had on a black dress," Cait said. "She was smiling and hugging you. Did you recognize her?"

I shook my head. "Never saw her before. Who do you think she is? New teacher or neighbor or something?"

Caitlyn shrugged. "She could be anybody. It's weird we both saw her, though."

"Yeah." I grinned. "What if it was our grand-mother?"

Cait stared at me. "Do you really think it could be? I mean, we're both probably thinking about her."

"Nah, I was just kidding. I bet it's not her. Especially since she probably lives somewhere overseas, at least judging by all the stamps on that box she sent us." I shrugged. "Anyway, these visions didn't seem to have anything to do with the pool party or the hospital or any of that. Let's try again and see if we can get something more useful."

She picked up the necklace, and we tried the same thing. But this time nothing happened.

It figured. If only we'd still had that letter— maybe it would tell us what to do. Or how to reach our grandmother.

"What now?" Caitlyn finally asked with a sigh.

I stared at her, feeling tired. "I don't know. We'll just have to keep trying to figure out those visions we had. Maybe try getting more from Bianca or the others?"

"Sounds like a plan." She smiled. "We might not

have much to go on. But at least we have each other, right?"

I rolled my eyes. "Sappy much?" I muttered.

But I couldn't help smiling back.

11
CAITLYN

"RELAX, WOULD YOU?" Cassie said as we walked into school the next morning. "It's not going to burn you."

"I know." I reached up and touched the necklace, which was tucked beneath the collar of my shirt. We'd decided I should be the one to wear it that day. So far our two scariest visions had been about Bianca, so it made sense to try to find out more from her.

A couple of seventh graders rushed past, talking excitedly about that weekend's football game. I cringed back against the wall, not wanting them to brush against me. Remembering how powerful that vision had been when I was wearing the necklace before made me nervous. Who knew what I might see now with its help?

"Chill," Cassie ordered, peering into my face. "Let me know if you find out anything interesting, okay?"

"For sure."

We parted ways to head to our lockers, which were at opposite ends of the school. As I reached mine, I heard someone calling my name. It was Liam—he and Bianca were coming toward me.

"Hey, Caitlyn," Liam greeted me in his usual cheerful way. "Only three days 'til the party!"

I smiled weakly, looking past him at Bianca. Maybe I could get this out of the way before homeroom.

"Yeah," I said. "Hey, Bianca, can you hold my books for a sec? My locker is kind of sticking."

"I'll do it." Liam grabbed my books.

As his hand brushed mine, the vision hit me hard.

A supervivid version of Liam appeared in front of me. He was soaking wet, dressed in swim trunks—and covered in blood! All four of the B Boys were dragging him across the cement deck of what I guessed had to be Megan's pool.

"Caitlyn!" The faded-out real Liam peered at me with concern, his voice barely breaking through the loud buzzing that filled my head. "Are you okay?"

"Give her some air—maybe she's overheated." Bianca yanked him back, abruptly breaking the connection.

I gasped, staggering forward and catching myself on my locker. "S-sorry," I blurted out. "I think you're right, Bianca. I must've walked too fast on the way here."

"Here, drink something." Liam pulled a water bottle out of his backpack.

"Thanks." I took a swig of the water, not meeting his eyes.

"It's hotter than ever out there today," Bianca said.

"Yeah." Liam grinned. "Which is another reason

I can't wait for that pool party."

I smiled weakly, then handed back the bottle. "Thanks," I said. "I, um, should go splash water on my face."

"Want me to come to the restroom with you?" Bianca offered.

"That's okay," I told her quickly. "I'll meet you guys in homeroom."

I slammed my locker door shut, then hurried down the hall in the direction of the girls' bathroom. Glancing back, I saw my friends walking the opposite way.

Good. I changed direction, heading for the stairs instead.

Soon I was poking my head into Cassie's homeroom. She was talking to Megan and a couple of their other friends. As soon as she saw my face, she excused herself and hurried out to meet me.

"What is it?" she asked, pulling me to a private spot in the hall behind a trash bin. "Did you get something from Bianca already?"

"Not Bianca." I took a deep breath, still shaken

by what I'd seen. "I had a vision about Liam."

"Liam?" She wrinkled her nose. "But—"

"Just listen," I cut her off, and I told her what I'd seen. "So now we know what's going to happen," I finished grimly. "The B Boys are going to beat him up so badly he'll end up in the hospital!"

Cassie shook her head. "No way," she said. "Those guys wouldn't do that."

"Are you sure?" I demanded. "They make fun of Liam all the time." I felt myself getting angry as I remembered the blood dripping down Liam's skinny torso. "Anyway, this explains the Bianca visions. She and Liam are friends—of course she'll be upset if he ends up in the hospital!"

"Yeah, okay." Cassie still didn't look convinced. "But there's got to be another explanation. Why would Lav and Megan be so upset?"

"Megan seems like a nice person," I said. "Besides, it happened—I mean, is going to happen—I mean, might happen . . ." I paused, realizing I was confusing myself.

"Okay, I get it," Cassie said. "You're right, Megan

would be upset. Especially if something happened at her house. But not Lavender. She was really crying hard in my vision."

She sounded very certain. I stared at her, wishing I could believe she was right. That Liam wasn't about to be beaten to a pulp at our birthday party. But what other explanation could there be?

"Speaking of Megan," Cassie added, glancing back into the classroom, "we were just talking about doing some shopping with Lav for the party after school today. So don't wait for me to walk home."

"But we need to talk about this!" I protested.

"We will," she assured me. "Tonight. I promise."

WHEN I GOT home, the front door was locked. "Guess Mom isn't home from work yet," I muttered as I fished for the key in my bag. For a second I couldn't find it, and I scowled, wishing Cassie hadn't ditched me to go off with her friends.

Then my fingers closed on the key, and relief washed over me. But I still felt annoyed with Cass. For one thing, we really did need to talk. Time was running out, and now that I'd seen what was going to happen, it seemed more important than ever to have a plan for how to stop it.

Besides, where did she get off going shopping for *our* party and not even inviting me? I could only imagine what kind of crazy stuff Lavender was talking her into buying right now.

But I wasn't going to worry about that. Not after what I'd seen today.

I grabbed a juice box out of the fridge, then wandered over to check the answering machine. There were no messages, just a missed call from someone the caller ID said was named Lockwood. The name seemed vaguely familiar, but I was too distracted to think about it much. I hit save so the name and number would stay on the machine for Mom, figuring it was probably one of her friends from her army days or something.

It had been extra hot and sticky that day, so I went to change into cooler clothes. As I pulled a tank top over my head, the key necklace clanked against my collarbone. I gasped, suddenly remembering where

I'd heard that name before.

"Lockwood!" I whispered, my heart beating faster. That was the name of the family I'd read about on the paranormal website. The ones who had the same type of power that Cassie and I did! Maybe someone had seen that post after all—maybe they were trying to contact me. I needed to get that phone number!

Racing out of my room, I skidded around the corner into the kitchen—and almost crashed into Mom. She was standing by the phone with a grim look on her face and her finger on the delete button.

"Wait!" I blurted out. "Don't erase that. I want to—"

Beep. The flashing light blinked off.

"No!" I collapsed against the counter, hardly believing this was happening. "Why did you do that?"

"It was clearly a wrong number." Mom pursed her lips and narrowed her eyes, as if challenging me to say anything else.

Normally that look was enough to make me

back off. But not today. Because why would she give me her best scarymama look over a simple wrong number?

"Are you sure?" I said, my heart beating a little faster. "You're sure you don't know anyone by that name—Lockwood?"

Mom frowned at me. "Where's Cassie?"

I wanted to repeat my question. Actually, I sort of wanted to scream and insist she tell me what was going on and why she was acting so weird about all this. That was what Cassie would have done.

But I wasn't Cassie. "Um, she went shopping," I said limply. "She'll be home soon."

Mom nodded and headed for the door. "I'll be in the shower."

12

CASSIE

"WELL?" CAITLYN DANCED around behind me, sounding anxious. "Are you getting anything?"

"Calm down." I bent closer to the answering machine. "I'm working on it."

For once, I was glad Mom was so old-fashioned. Because that meant we actually still had one of those old-school cordless phones with a built-in answering machine. It meant we had a shot at retrieving that number.

"I wish I'd recognized the name right away,"

Cait moaned. "I could've written down the number before Mom even got home."

"Yeah, I wish you had, too," I said. "Are you sure it's the right name?"

She nodded. "Lockwood. I'm almost positive that's the name from that website." She checked the clock on the microwave. "Hurry," she urged. "We have to leave soon or we'll be late for school."

"Relax." I continued to fiddle with the recorder thingy. I'm pretty handy with machines and tech, and Cait and I were both hoping I could figure out how to retrieve a deleted number.

But nothing I tried seemed to work. "Well?" Cait said as I straightened up and sighed.

"Nada," I replied. "Sorry. I think it's hopeless."

Caitlyn looked disappointed, verging on devastated. "Do you think they'll call again?"

"Your guess is as good as mine." I glanced at her. "Are you wearing the necklace?"

"No. That thing kind of scares me." She shivered. "Why don't you wear it today?"

I rolled my eyes. "Fine, scaredy-cat. I will."

Actually, I didn't blame her for being freaked out, now that we knew the talisman might be connected to our visions. I was a little freaked out, too, especially when I remembered those extra-vivid visions I'd had while wearing it.

But I wasn't about to admit that to her.

"SETTLE DOWN, YOUNG scholars." Ms. Xavier clapped her hands to bring the class to order.

I'd been chatting with Megan and the minions. Megan sat right in front of me, and I'd taken every opportunity to brush against her, touch her on the arm, whatever. I was getting nothing. No visions, zilch, a big fat zippo.

As Ms. X started babbling on about our research projects, I glanced over my shoulder at Brayden, who sat a couple of rows behind me. If what Cait had seen was true, maybe he was the one I should be trying to touch.

The thought made my face go hot. I stared at the teacher, hoping nobody noticed.

". . . so you'll have a free period today to continue

your preliminary research and outlining," Ms. X was saying. "I'd like you all to try to settle on your final topics by the end of next week at the latest, all right? Now go forth and research!"

Most people pulled out their smartphones to go on the Internet. Others hopped up and headed for the bookshelves or the classroom computer.

I just sat there trying to focus. With everything else that had been going on, I'd barely spent two seconds thinking about this stupid project.

Then I noticed Ms. X heading toward me with a big smile on her face. Uh-oh.

"Cassie," she said. "Have you and Caitlyn discussed pursuing my idea?"

"Um, sort of," I said. "It sounds cool and all, but Cait really has her heart set on doing her own thing, so . . ."

"Oh, are you sure?" she said. "As I mentioned, I'd be happy to guide you two, help you figure out the best way to explore all the facets of your twinhood."

She looked really disappointed, which kind of

weirded me out. Why was she so into this twin thing, anyway?

Then again, why did she feel the need to wear a ring on each finger and a dozen bracelets on each arm? She was an oddball, that was why. Case closed.

She leaned on my desk, gazing earnestly into my face. "Cassie," she said. "This project could be very useful to you and your sister. It could help you open up new possibilities, maybe discover new things about yourself. Help you explore the true power of being twins."

I forced a smile, though I was more weirded out than ever. This went beyond oddballness. Was it possible that she suspected something was going on with us?

No—that's crazy talk, I told myself sternly. There's no way she knows anything. She probably just saw a cheesy made-for-TV movie about twin telepaths or something, and thinks she's going to help us discover how to read each other's minds.

And reading Caitlyn's mind? Not really something I aspired to. I had no interest in learning her deepest thoughts about rainbows and puppies and pink-frosted cupcakes. Or whatever she thought about all day.

"Um," I began, not sure what to say to Ms. Xavier.

She put a hand on my shoulder. "Just tell me you'll talk to her once more, all right?" she said.

At least I was pretty sure that's what she said. I couldn't be positive, since my brain was suddenly full of buzzing as a vision slammed into my head.

The vision showed Ms. Xavier, of course. She was in her classroom, pretty much right where she was standing now. Only the place was empty except for me and Cait. We were standing in front of the teacher, who was smiling and looking excited.

Just then minion Abby called out to Ms. X, wanting help with something or other. The teacher moved away, and the vision disappeared. I flopped back in my seat, my heart racing.

Okay, that one didn't look too bad, I told myself. Maybe Cait was right—maybe not everything I see is something terrible.

Then another possibility occurred to me.

Or maybe it just means Ms. Xavier is going to successfully browbeat us into doing her stupid project idea, I thought with a grimace. *That would probably qualify as a bad thing.*

But a big waste of a vision. There were more important things to think about than that stupid project. That was one of the most aggravating parts of this whole Sight. We seemed to have no control over what kinds of things we saw. Sometimes it was completely trivial stuff, like seeing a grade on a test ahead of time. Other times? Majorly important stuff. Like Mom almost losing her job. Or Liam covered in blood at our birthday party.

My gaze wandered to Brayden, who was bent over his notebook scribbling busily. Had Cait really seen what she thought she had? Could Brayden and his friends really be capable of something like that?

It was hard to believe. But if it did happen, we needed to be ready. No question about it.

13
CAITLYN

WHEN I WOKE up on Friday morning, I couldn't remember exactly why I was filled with dread and anxiety.

Then it hit me. One more day until the party.

I lay there in bed with my eyes closed, trying not to picture what I'd seen in my visions. Liam covered in blood. The B Boys dragging him along like a limp rag doll. Bianca sobbing in the hospital waiting room.

With a shudder, I opened my eyes and looked over at the other bed. It was empty. I heard the sound of the shower from across the hall.

Mom poked her head in. "Up and at 'em, Cait," she said. "Breakfast is on."

"Coming." I climbed out of bed and headed for the kitchen.

Since Mom was around, Cassie and I didn't have a chance to talk until we left the house. For once I was glad for the long, hot walk to school.

"Any new ideas?" I asked as we trudged along.

"Not really. You?"

"No." She'd told me about her latest vision, of course. Even though it didn't seem connected to the rest, it just added to my anxiety. "Maybe we should cancel. We could blame it on Mom, say we got in trouble and she grounded us."

"We can't," Cassie responded immediately. "The party's tomorrow, and everyone is superpsyched. It'd be social suicide to call it off now."

"But—" I began.

"But that's not all," she cut me off. "Megan is in full-out hostess mode, and Lav is in a frenzy, decorating and planning food and stuff. Even if we pulled out, I bet the party would go on without us."

"But would Liam still be invited?" I countered.

She glanced at me. "If Lav had her say? No way. But Megan's different. She'd still let everyone come."

I sighed, knowing she was right. The party train had already left the station, and it was way too late to stop it now. All we could do was try to prevent it from crashing.

"Okay, then we have to figure out what we're going to do," I said.

"I was thinking about that." She kicked at a stone on the sidewalk. "At this point, it seems like our only option is to play defense. You make sure Liam is never out of your sight, and I stick close to the B Boys."

Despite the serious situation, I couldn't help smirking. "That's awfully selfless of you," I said. "I'm sure it will be terrible for you to be forced to spend tons of time with that cute Brayden Diaz."

She shot me a scowl. "Grow up, Caitlyn."

I grinned. Clearly I'd struck a nerve. Once this was over, I was going to have to figure out what was going on with Cassie and Brayden.

My smile faded as I saw the school looming on the horizon. "Anyway, it's the best plan we've got so far. Let's keep thinking, though."

I WALKED INTO homeroom. Ms. Xavier was standing at her desk shuffling through some papers. Most of the other kids were there, too, including Liam. He was bent over some homework in his usual seat in the first row.

"Where's Bianca?" I asked as I took my seat beside him.

He looked up from his homework. "Not here yet, I guess," he said. "I thought maybe you weren't going to show up either. Ms. X never gets here before you do."

"I know. Cass and I left a little late this morning." I sat down and glanced at Bianca's empty desk. "It's not like Bianca to be late, though. Do you think she missed her bus?"

Liam shrugged. "There's a first time for everything."

He didn't seem concerned, but that empty seat was giving me a bad feeling.

Don't jump to conclusions, I told myself. *She probably has a dentist appointment she forgot to mention to us or something.*

"So are you all ready for the party?" Liam asked. "I looked at the weather report this morning, and it's supposed to be hot again tomorrow."

I forced a smile. "Yeah, the weather should be perfect."

"It must be weird," he said with his loud, snorty laugh. "Having your birthday this time of year, you're probably not used to having a pool party, right?"

Ms. Xavier looked up sharply. She took a step toward us.

"Birthday?" she said with interest. "Is your birthday coming up, Caitlyn?"

"It's tomorrow," I told her, still distracted by Bianca's empty seat.

Ms. Xavier raised an eyebrow. "I see!" she exclaimed. "Have you noticed anything strange this week?"

"Strange?" I blinked at her. "What do you mean?"

She smiled. "I've heard that birthdays can be times of exaggerated mental and emotional power for some people—especially twins. That's something you could explore in your report, perhaps?"

Was she ever going to give it a rest? I wasn't particularly interested in doing my report on being a twin, especially right now. And even if Cassie and I didn't really have *twintuition*, I was pretty sure she felt the same way.

"Did you know that William Shakespeare died on his birthday?" Liam said. "He wasn't even that old."

In the short time I'd known him, I'd already discovered that Liam was full of random facts like that. And that he liked to share them pretty much anytime. Usually I found it charming, but now I sort of wished he'd pulled out a more cheerful fact to share.

"Fascinating," Ms. Xavier said. Then she glanced at me. "Happy birthday, Caitlyn. I'll have to be sure to wish Cassie the same when I see her in class later."

She turned away and called the class to order

for morning announcements. I sat there staring into space and thinking about what she'd said. According to the post on that message board, members of the Lockwood family came into their powers when they turned twelve. So it seemed birthdays did have some sort of special significance, at least for people like Cassie and me. Could Ms. Xavier possibly know that? All this time I'd been writing her off as a kook. But maybe it was worth talking to her, finding out if she'd ever heard of the Sight, or the Lockwoods, or any of the rest of it.

As I tried to imagine how that conversation would go, I winced. No, I was just grasping at straws. Our best bet to find out what was happening to us was our grandmother. Once the party was over, Cassie and I would have to track her down. Even though Mom seemed determined to stonewall us forever.

The bell rang, and I glanced at Bianca's still-empty seat. She was officially tardy now. Was it weird that she'd pulled a no-show today of all days? Or just a coincidence?

"Are you sure Bianca didn't mention anything about being absent today?" I whispered to Liam.

He shrugged. "I don't think so. Maybe she's sick."

Sick enough to end up in the hospital? I wondered.

I slumped down in my seat with a sigh, wondering if Cassie had been right all along. Seeing the future had seemed kind of fun at first. Like a cool superpower from a movie. But lately it was starting to feel like a whole lot of trouble.

"WHY DIDN'T YOU call her if you're so worried?" Cassie said as she climbed into bed that night.

"I sent her a text at lunchtime, but I never heard back." Bianca hadn't showed up at all that day. Liam had texted her, too, reminding her about the pool party. Neither of us had received a response. Liam hadn't seemed worried, but he didn't know better. He hadn't seen what I had.

But somehow Cassie didn't seem particularly worried either. "Bianca wasn't hurt in any of our visions. We need to focus on the real problem."

"Liam," I agreed. "I just wish we knew more about what was going to happen. And when."

"We know when. We just have to keep the B Boys away from Liam at the party, and we're golden."

She made it sound so easy. Then again, she hadn't been the one who'd seen that terrible vision of Liam with blood all over him.

"It's not much of a plan," I fretted.

"It's the only one we've got. Anyway, it can work." She yawned and switched off her bedside lamp. "We changed the future before, right? We can do it again."

"Since when are you Miss Optimistic?" I said with a ghost of a smile. "I thought that was my job."

She grinned at me in the darkness. "I learned from the best."

"Ha-ha," I said. "Okay, let's hope for the best, then. I'm good at that, right?"

Wrong. As soon as I closed my eyes it was there—the image of Liam from my vision. Could we really stop it from coming true?

At least Cassie is fully on board with helping this

time, I thought as sleep crowded the corners of my mind. *I know I can count on her to help keep an eye on things tomorrow. And at least this time we know exactly what's coming.*

14
CASSIE

"HAPPY BIRTHDAY TO my favorite twins!" Mom sang out as Caitlyn and I walked into the kitchen the next morning. She had an apron tied on over her jeans and T-shirt, and she was wielding a spatula.

I blinked at her, wondering if I was still asleep and dreaming. Because Mom hadn't been this chipper in days—maybe weeks. Come to think of it, I wasn't sure she'd *ever* been this chipper.

"Thanks," Caitlyn said, hurrying over to give her a hug.

"I made pancakes," Mom said. "Chocolate chip for Cassie and banana walnut for Cait."

"My favorite!" Caitlyn exclaimed.

"Thanks, Mom," I said, sitting down. "Smells great." I tried to muster some enthusiasm, but it felt fake. How could Mom act as if this were a totally ordinary birthday? How could she pretend that nothing was wrong?

Still, I knew it wouldn't do any good to antagonize her, especially not today. She'd taken off work to help Megan's folks chaperone the party, so I'd have to deal with plenty of blowback if I annoyed her now.

"Good, good." Mom sort of hovered there, waving the spatula around aimlessly, almost nervously. It must have been my imagination, though, because Mom didn't get nervous, pretty much ever.

"What's this?" Caitlyn reached for a shopping bag in the middle of the table.

"Oh! I almost forgot." Mom smiled. "Those are your birthday presents. Go ahead—open them."

There were several gifts for each of us. Once

again, I played along, gushing over the flip-flops and bracelet she'd gotten me. Okay, the bracelet really was pretty sweet. At the bottom of the bag were envelopes from our Maw Maw Jean and various other relatives on Mom's side. Mine contained a hefty gift certificate to my favorite store. Again, sweet.

But it was hard to enjoy it, since thinking of Maw Maw Jean just reminded me of my other grandmother, the one I'd never met, whose name I didn't even know.

I wolfed down my stack of pancakes, then pushed back from the table. "Dibs on first shower," I told Cait. "We should get moving—I told Megan we'd be there by ten to help set up."

A few minutes later, I was clean and dressed in my swimsuit and a pair of shorts. As I pulled a tee on over my suit, the key-shaped pendant caught my eye. It was lying on the dresser, where I'd put it last night.

Yanking the shirt the rest of the way on, I grabbed the necklace. I stared at it, hesitating only briefly before putting it on and tucking it under the collar of my shirt.

"WOW," CAIT MURMURED as we pulled through a set of tall iron gates. "Nice place!"

Major understatement. This was my first time at Megan's house, and it was even fancier than I'd expected. A long, curving drive led between rows of huge oak trees. The house was enormous, pale stucco with lots of windows and scrolled pillars holding up the portico.

"Here we are," Mom said, stopping in front of the entrance. She was still in cheerful mode. "Help me get the stuff out of the trunk."

We were unloading bags of food and soda when Megan and Lavender emerged from the house and rushed toward us. Frisking around their legs was a brown-and-white dog on a long leash, the other end of which was looped around Lavender's arm. I gasped. It was the dog from my vision!

Caitlyn noticed my reaction and raised her eyebrows. I nodded slightly, then bent to pat the dog as it strained forward to greet us, tail wagging nonstop.

"You're here!" Megan cried. "Come on in. We've got most of the decorations done, but we still need to blow up more balloons and make the punch."

"Who's this?" I tried to sound casual as I rubbed the friendly dog's ears.

"This is Amigo," Lavender replied. "He's helping, too."

Amigo? Of course—I should have guessed. According to the rest of our friends, Lavender was a total animal freak. Since her parents wouldn't let her fill the house with critters, Lav doted on her dog. You know those annoying parents who talk about their kids like they're the second coming? That was Lav whenever she mentioned Amigo.

The front door swung open again, and a tall, slender blond woman hurried out. "Welcome!" she exclaimed, offering Mom her hand. "You must be Deidre Waters. I've heard so many lovely things about you!"

Mom smiled and shook her hand. "Hello, Mayor March. It's great to finally meet you."

Mrs. March's laugh sounded like tinkling bells. "Please! Call me Renee. I may be the mayor at work, but around here I barely qualify as human, let alone any kind of authority figure." She winked. "You have tweens, too, so I know you hear me on that."

"I do." Mom chuckled. "Thanks so much for hosting this party. It's very generous of you."

"Oh, it's nothing." Mrs. March waved a hand. "Here, let me help you bring your things inside."

The two of them grabbed more bags out of the trunk and headed for the house, chatting like old friends. "Wow," Caitlyn said to Megan. "Your mom seems great."

Megan shrugged. "I guess. Come on, I'll show you guys the pool. It's out back."

She headed toward the front door, but Lavender stopped her. "Let's take the scenic route," she said. "Otherwise your mom will want to play twenty questions with the twins once she gets through with their mother." She jerked her head toward Cait and me.

"Good point." Megan smiled at us. "Mom is a

true politician. She loves talking to people—a little too much sometimes. Come on, we'll go this way."

We followed her around to the side of the house, carrying the rest of the bags. Amigo raced between our legs, dashing around as much as the leash would let him and barking at passing birds. We passed through a sturdy gate built into a tall plank fence. Inside, nestled up against the side wall of the house, was a grassy area dotted with small, carefully pruned trees. A cluster of potted plants sat in a sunny spot near a door leading inside. The fenced area was probably at least twice the size of our backyard, though next to the rest of Megan's place it seemed small.

I recognized it right away—this little private garden at the side of the house. It was in my vision about Megan and Amigo. Go figure—for once maybe I really had seen something pleasant, like Cait said! In any case, the place looked just as peaceful and pretty as it had in my vision.

"Dad calls this the orchard," Megan explained, gesturing at the trees. "It's sort of his hobby."

"Yeah." Lavender laughed. "If you're wondering why it looks like Fort Knox, it's because he's always trying to keep the deer and raccoons and birds from eating the fruit. Next he'll probably buy a cannon to scare them off."

Megan giggled. "I think I saw a cannon catalog lying around the house. Don't tell the neighbors."

"I won't have to," Lav countered. "We'll be able to hear it all the way over at my house."

I smiled, but at the same time I felt a tiny bit left out. These two had obviously been friends for ages. I'd started to feel more at home in Aura the past few weeks, but suddenly I was back to feeling like an outsider.

Then Megan turned her sunny smile on me. "I'm so glad you're having your party here, you two," she said. "It's going to be fun."

That made me feel better. At least about the friendship thing. But fun? I could only cross my fingers and hope it was true. Liam hadn't seemed to be having much fun in Caitlyn's vision. Catching her eye, I guessed that she was thinking the same thing.

"So where's this pool, anyway?" I said to cover my weird mood.

"Right back here." Megan hurried ahead and flipped the latch on a second gate. The sound of music drifted toward us, along with the smell of chlorine.

"Wow," Caitlyn said.

I knew how she felt. The pool area was just like I'd seen it in my vision —nicer than anywhere we'd celebrated our birthday before.

For a while we were so busy that I barely had time to breathe, let alone worry about the future. Megan and Lavender had already set up a bunch of stuff on a big teak table. We added our food, then helped finish the decorations and mix a huge volume of frothy pink fruit punch in Mrs. March's enormous crystal punch bowl.

Finally Megan seemed satisfied. She glanced around, tapping her chin. "I think we're ready."

"Just in time." Lavender checked her watch. "People should be getting here soon. I'd better put

Amigo away." She'd let the dog off the leash in the fenced-in pool area while we set up. Now she clipped the leash back on. "Can I put him in the orchard?" she asked Megan. "He'll be out of the way there, and he can take a nice nap in the shade."

"Aw, can't he come to the party?" Caitlyn patted the happy little dog as his butt wiggled with enthusiasm.

"I'll probably bring him out to say hi later," Lav said. "I just want him out of the way while everyone's arriving. Otherwise he's likely to run out through the house and chase a squirrel into the road or something."

"Yeah." Megan smiled. "He's incorrigible. Aren't you, boy?"

Amigo practically turned himself inside out with joy as Megan patted him. Then Lav gave a tug on the leash. "Okay, that's enough. Into solitary with you, baby."

She picked up the dog and snuggled him. Then she disappeared into the orchard.

"I'll make sure Mom is ready for our visitors,"

Megan said. "Be right back."

She hurried into the house, leaving me and Caitlyn alone.

"It's weird being here, isn't it?" Cait said with a wry smile. "It's our first time seeing everything. Only not."

"I know, right?" I glanced toward the pool, shuddering as the image of my sobbing friends swam into my mind. "Definitely weird."

I forgot about that when Mom emerged through the open French doors. "Everything ready to go out here?" she asked.

"I think so," Cait told her. "People should start arriving any minute."

"Good." Mom hesitated, glancing from my sister to me and back again. She cleared her throat, and once again I couldn't help thinking she looked nervous. "Listen, girls, while we have a moment alone . . ."

At that moment Lavender raced back into view, kicking the orchard gate shut behind her. "They're here!" she squealed.

"Who?" I asked.

Megan hurried back out just in time to hear her. She rolled her eyes and smiled. "The B Boys," she said. "Leave it to them to be fashionably early, right?"

Lav laughed breathlessly. "How's my hair?"

"Looks good." I glanced at Mom out of the corner of my eye. What had she been about to say? After everything that had been going on, I really wanted to know.

She caught my look and stepped toward me. "Happy birthday, Cassie," she said, giving me a quick hug.

I didn't hug her back. I couldn't. It was all I could do to stay on my feet as the vision hit me.

Even though the real Mom was right in my face, I could hardly see her. All I could see was future Mom, superclear—and superangry. This was scary-mama times infinity—she was scowling so hard she almost looked like a whole different person.

Mom let me go and stepped away to hug Cait. I just stood there, shaking. What had made future Mom so angry? I had no idea—for once, I'd barely been able to see any background aside from a plain white wall. I hadn't even been able to tell what Mom was wearing.

Oh, well, I thought, doing my best to shrug it off. She was probably mad at Cait for not making the bed again. Or me for coming home half a second past curfew.

In any case, the wall told me the scene, whatever it was, would take place indoors. The walls I could see through the numerous windows were all shades of tasteful pastel. Mayor Megan's Mom didn't seem like a plain-white-walls kind of person.

That meant I could worry about this newest vision later. Right now I needed to focus on our visions about this party.

As Mom hurried toward the house, I touched the pendant around my neck. Suddenly I didn't want to wear it anymore. I was going to have enough to deal with today without any more random superstrong visions.

Pulling it off, I slipped it to Cait. "Here," I murmured. "You can wear this, okay?"

She hesitated, then nodded and took it from me. Relieved, I turned back to my friends.

"Chill out, Lav," Megan was saying. "A girl should never look desperate, you know."

Caitlyn looked confused. "Desperate?" she echoed as she slipped the necklace over her head.

"Oh, didn't you hear?" Megan smiled. "Lav just decided she has a massive crush on Biff."

"Really?" That got my attention. Last I'd noticed, Lavender had seemed to be crushing on Brayden. Which was sort of a problem, given my own weird, mixed-up feelings about him. "Why didn't you tell me about this before?"

"Shut up, Megs. You don't have to tell the whole world my business." But Lavender was grinning like an idiot as she shoved Megan. "Now be quiet, guys. Here they come!"

Brent and Buzz bounded out through the French doors. "Yo, the party can start!" Brent exclaimed. "We're here!"

Biff and Brayden were right behind them. Biff was carrying two towels and helping Brayden maneuver his crutches down the wide, curved steps leading from the house to the pool area.

"I hope there's lots of food," Buzz said. "Swimming makes me hungry!"

Biff laughed. "Dude, when did a party of Megan's ever not have tons of food?" Dropping the towels on a lounge chair, he hurried over and grabbed a handful of chips.

Meanwhile Brayden hobbled toward us. "Hey," he said. "Thanks for inviting us. Happy birthday."

He smiled at both me and Cait but held my gaze for an extra second.

I grinned back at him, glad that I'd volunteered to stick close to the B Boys today. "Thanks," I said. "Now come on and let's get this party started!"

15
CAITLYN

THE PARTY HAD been in full swing for almost an hour before Bianca finally showed up. I was relieved when she stepped out through the French doors.

"You made it!" I cried, hurrying to greet her.

She handed me a small, brightly wrapped gift. "Happy birthday, Caitlyn. Thanks for inviting me. This looks like quite a party." She shaded her eyes and glanced toward the pool.

There had to be at least thirty kids there. Some were lounging on the teak chaises, some were picking at the food, a few were dancing to the loud pop music pouring out of the fancy speakers attached to Megan's smartphone. Lots more were in the pool splashing around.

I'd been in and out of the pool a few times myself. Liam had arrived only moments after the B Boys, and I'd stuck close to him ever since. He was so excited he couldn't seem to settle on one activity.

Glancing over my shoulder, I saw that he was hanging out by the food table gorging on Mom's homemade cookies. The B Boys were all in the pool except for Brayden, who was watching his friends from nearby with his cast propped up on a chair. As I watched, Buzz hoisted himself out, then turned around and cannonballed right back in, almost landing on a laughing Biff. Cassie was floating nearby, smiling at the guys' antics.

"Sorry I'm late." When Bianca turned to face me again, I couldn't help noticing that her eyes were red and puffy.

"Are you okay?" I blurted out. "You look like you've been crying."

Okay, maybe not the most tactful question. What can I say? I was worried about her.

"I was. But it's okay." Her smile widened. "You haven't known me that long, but I never cry when I'm upset—only when I'm really, really happy."

"Really?" I was a little confused but relieved. "What are you happy about?"

"I just came from the hospital. My dad had heart surgery yesterday."

I gasped. "He did?" That explained why she hadn't been at school. "What happened? Is he okay?"

"He's good. Great, actually." She beamed. "His doctors said the surgery went perfectly, and he'll be a lot healthier now."

"Oh, Bianca, that's amazing!" I grabbed her in a big hug.

She hugged me back, laughing. "Anyway, sorry if I've been a little quiet lately. I was just worried about him, you know?"

I didn't bother to point out that she was always quiet. All that mattered was that her dad was okay.

Wait. Maybe that wasn't all that mattered.

"Go grab some snacks before Liam eats everything," I urged. "I'll join you in a sec. I just have to find my sister first."

As she nodded and hurried off, I headed toward Cassie, who was now sitting on the edge of the pool near Brayden's chair, grinning as Biff and Buzz tried to dunk a laughing, struggling Brent nearby.

When I got closer, I shot her a meaningful look. "Can I talk to you for a minute?"

She stood up immediately. "Be right back," she told Brayden.

I led the way to a quiet spot behind the waterfall. "Guess what?" I said as soon as we were alone. "Bianca's dad had heart trouble!"

She looked startled. "And this makes you happy why?"

"Sorry!" I laughed. "Let me start over." I filled her in on what I'd found out. "So I'm guessing your vision was Bianca going to the hospital before surgery yesterday. You said she looked worried, right? And mine showed her crying with happiness after she found out he was going to be okay."

"Yeah. Go figure. Turns out my vision is the negative one and yours is all happy happy joy joy. Again."

"Oh. Right." I shrugged. "But this is great news for both of us! Now that we don't have to worry about Bianca anymore, we can finally relax and enjoy our party!"

"Not exactly," she pointed out. "What about Liam? And the thing I saw with Lav and the girls crying. Neither of those visions have happened yet, and they both definitely took place right here at this pool."

My heart dropped. I'd been so distracted by the whole Bianca thing that I'd almost forgotten about Liam. Where was he now?

I peered out around the waterfall. The last time I'd seen him, Liam had been at the food table. He wasn't there now, though.

Then I heard a shout. Turning my head, I gasped as I saw Liam over near the deep end with the B Boys. They were all laughing, including Liam. But for how long? My heart thudded, and I took a step forward.

"Geronimo!" Buzz shouted, racing toward the water. When he reached the edge of the pool, he leaped up and forward, grabbing his knees and landing with a loud splash.

"Hey!" Emily and Abby shrieked as the wave from Buzz's cannonball washed over them.

"I'm next!" Liam cried with a wild laugh.

He took off, running the same way Buzz just had. But someone had left a towel lying on the ground, and Liam's foot snagged it. He tripped and went flying, his skinny arms and legs windmilling helplessly.

"Aaaah—ow!" he yelped as he hit the ground stomach first, the momentum carrying him forward over the rough concrete.

"Liam!" I yelled.

"Dude!" one or two of the B Boys exclaimed at the same time.

Liam finally stopped just short of the pool's edge, rolling over with a moan. His chest and stomach were scraped and bleeding, the blood mixing with the water dripping from his hair and body.

"That hurt," he announced, staring up at the sky.

"We've got you, bro!" Biff and Brent had reached him by now, while Buzz was climbing out of the pool.

"We've got to . . ." I began, stepping forward.

Then I stopped, blinking in amazement as the scene from my vision formed in front of my eyes. Biff pulled Liam to his feet, while Brent slung one of Liam's skinny arms over his own broad shoulder. With Buzz tailing along, the guys dragged the blood-streaked Liam toward the nearest lounge chair.

Lavender was sitting there drinking a soda. Her eyes widened when she saw the boys coming.

"Ew!" she exclaimed, leaping out of the way. "Don't bleed on me!"

"Sorry." Liam grinned at her. "I'm afraid I don't have control over my bleeding. See, it's what's called an involuntary reflex, which I believe is controlled by the central nervous system—or is it the peripheral nervous system . . . ?"

As he babbled on, I went limp with relief. Yeah, he might look like an ax murderer had taken a swing at him, but I had a feeling he was going to be okay.

I glanced over at Cassie, who looked confused. "I don't get it," she said. "Your vision . . ."

"Right." I let out a breath quickly. "I saw Liam bleeding and those guys dragging him along. I thought it meant they'd, you know, caused the bleeding. But I guess not."

"Yeah. It was Liam's own spazziness that did that." She wandered off. "Come on, we should probably check on him. He's going to need a whole box of Band-Aids."

By the time we reached Liam, most of the party had gathered around. Megan ran for her mother. Mrs. March took one look at Liam, clucked with concern, then went into commanding-general mode.

"Megan, honey, run out and grab me the Adams General bag from the front seat of my car, okay?" she said. "I noticed we ran out of Band-Aids the other day, and I picked some up in town this morning. On your way back, swing through the orchard and fetch me some aloe from the big clay pot."

She disappeared into the house with Liam in

tow. Megan bolted after them. The B Boys tagged along, still looking concerned.

"Wow," Lavender said, wandering toward us. "Drama much? Your friends sure know how to keep things interesting, Caitlyn."

"Yeah." I barely heard her. I headed for the house, wanting to check on Liam.

Cassie followed. As soon as we were inside, she yanked me into the powder room near the French doors.

"What?" I said, distracted. "I want to make sure Liam's okay."

"He's fine," Cassie said. "I mean, I'm sure he's hurting after that pavement dive he took. But Megan's mom used to be a nurse—she'll get him fixed up."

"Good." That actually did make me feel better. Still, I wanted to see for myself. "I'll go check on him and let you know, okay? You might as well go enjoy the party now that everything's happened."

"But it hasn't. What about Lavender?"

"What about her?"

"I saw her crying. Right here at the pool." She bit

her lip. "Wearing the same swimsuit she's wearing today."

"Whatever." I shrugged. "She's probably heart-broken because she smudged her lip gloss or something. Or maybe Liam did manage to drip some blood on her fancy swimsuit and it's the biggest tragedy of her life."

Cassie grimaced. "Maybe," she admitted. "I don't know, though. Everyone in the vision looked upset, not just Lav. Especially Megan."

She had a point. But what else could possibly happen today? Especially something that could upset everyone so much?

I scanned back over all the visions I'd had lately, but came up with nothing. They'd all come true except the ones about Mom and the gray-haired lady. And obviously those didn't have anything to do with today's party.

So why hadn't Cassie's crying vision happened yet? Had we prevented it somehow without even realizing it? But how? There had to be a clue some-where . . .

"Wait," I blurted out. "You had a vision about Megan, right?"

She frowned impatiently. "Aren't you listening? I just said she was in the background of my Lavender vision."

"No, another one," I said. "With a dog."

Cassie's eyes widened. "You're right!" she cried, leaping for the door. "Hurry, we have to get out there—I think I know what's going to happen!"

16
CASSIE

CAITLYN FOLLOWED AS I raced outside and around the corner. She'd reminded me of that vision of Megan and Amigo in the orchard, and now I was pretty sure I knew what it meant. I'd seen Megan coming in through the front gate, the one leading out to the driveway—and the busy street just beyond.

There was just one question: Was I too late to save Amigo?

I shoved through the back gate into the orchard. Megan was on the far side, holding a plastic bag and bending down to rub Amigo's ears as he leaped happily around her. The gate behind her was standing ajar.

"Megan!" I hollered. "The gate!"

"Huh?" She straightened up and peered at me.

Caitlyn gasped. "Oh, no—he's escaping!"

Amigo had just spotted the open gate and was charging toward it. "Amigo!" I cried. "Stop!"

He ignored me, his wagging tail disappearing through the gate. Megan spun around.

"No!" she cried. "Oh, no! Amigo!"

She dropped the bag and leaped back through the gate. I sprinted across the orchard with Cait on my heels. We emerged just in time to see Amigo playing keepaway with Megan. Namely, he was keeping himself just out of arm's reach, his little tail wagging nonstop.

I glanced toward the road just in time to see a huge delivery truck rumble past. Yikes. If the dog headed that direction . . .

"Go that way," I ordered Caitlyn. "I'll circle around and try to cut him off."

Cait nodded and took off to Megan's right, while I headed left. Meanwhile Megan kept grabbing frantically at Amigo, and he kept leaping away at the last second. What if he took off after a squirrel or something?

No. I wouldn't let that happen. Banishing the image of Lav's tear-streaked face, I slowed down, creeping up behind the dog. He was distracted by Megan pleading with him to stop. If I could just get a tiny bit closer . . .

"Gotcha!" I yelled as I grabbed the little dog.

Amigo whined with surprise. But as I hugged him to me, he started wiggling and wagging his tail again, and his tongue lolled out and then slurped me right across the face.

Gross. But, okay, kind of sweet.

A breathless Megan rushed over. "Amigo, you naughty thing!" she exclaimed. "Thanks for helping me catch him, Cassie. I was in such a hurry to get Mom the stuff she needs, I forgot to check that the gate was shut. If Amigo had gotten into the road . . ." She shuddered.

I sank to my knees, still hugging Amigo. Closing my eyes, I once again pictured Lavender's distraught, tear-streaked face from my vision. The face of a dog-loving girl whose best furry friend had just been hit by a car.

"I'd better get the aloe and get inside," Megan said. Her moment of distress had passed. She didn't know how close she'd really come to ruining Lavender's life and destroying their friendship.

I stood and followed her back into the orchard, still holding Amigo. Caitlyn came, too. We both watched Megan pluck a stem off a weird-looking plant, then push through the gate into the pool area.

Cait patted Amigo as I set him down—after double-checking the front gate. "So that's what you saw," she said. "Megan accidentally letting the dog out in the road."

"Yeah." I wiped dog drool off my chin and stood up. "As soon as you mentioned my vision, I suddenly got it. It was the only thing that made sense. Lav adores this dog. She'd be devastated if anything happened to him."

That also explained why Megan had been behind the other girls in my vision, crying by herself. Lavender had probably blamed her for what had happened to Amigo.

What had *almost* happened to Amigo, that is. Glancing down at the lively little dog, I smiled with relief.

"So we did it," I said. "We changed the future. Again."

Caitlyn nodded. "And something else happened again," she said. "A vision you thought was good turned out to be bad. I mean, here you thought it was just a nice vision of Megan petting Amigo, right?"

"Gee, thanks for pointing that out, sis." I rolled my eyes. "I love being reminded of what a downer my visions are."

"No, but listen," she said. "It's a good thing you see bad stuff, right? Because that gives us a chance to stop it!"

I thought about that for a second. Maybe she had a point. Maybe my bad visions were actually more important than her good ones. Not that I was about to admit it.

"Okay," I said. "Anyway, like you said, we don't know for sure that I only see bad stuff and you only see good stuff. What about your Liam vision?"

"But that didn't turn out so bad, did it?" Cait said. "I mean, yeah, those scrapes couldn't have felt good. But the main thing my vision focused on was the B Boys, remember? The good thing was the way they all rushed to help Liam." She smiled. "Which is great, right? It shows that they're good guys, even if they do mess with people sometimes."

"If you say so." Just then a shout of laughter drifted in from the direction of the pool. "But let's not waste time with philosophy or whatever, okay? Now that we've saved the day, let's get in there and enjoy our birthday party!"

HOURS LATER, THE party was winding down. Some people had left already, though the B Boys were still there. Brayden was on a lounge chair chatting with a bandaged-up but cheerful—and slightly sunburned—Liam, while the other three played keepaway with a beach ball in the pool.

I wandered over to the food table, where Megan was tidying up. "Thanks again for all this," I said.

"You're welcome." She smiled at me. "Happy birthday, Cassie."

"Thanks." I grabbed a leftover cookie. "You sure know how to throw one seriously epic party! I bet it's the talk of the school on Monday."

She laughed, then frowned slightly. "That reminds me," she said slowly. "Did you say anything about the party to Gabe Campbell?"

"Ew, no." I made a face. "He's about the last person I'd want to invite. Why?"

"Because I ran into him on the way out of school yesterday." Megan wiped some crumbs off the table. "He was asking all kinds of questions about you and your birthday and stuff like that." She shrugged. "Probably no biggie. He's always been kind of strange, you know?"

"Yeah." But I couldn't help feeling uneasy as I

remembered coming out of that classroom to find him watching us the other day. "No biggie."

Before I could say anything else, Brayden was coming toward us, swinging along on his crutches. "Hey," he said. "Thanks for everything, Megan. And happy birthday, Cassie. Thanks for inviting me."

"No problem." I tried to sound casual. "I'm glad you came. You know—all you guys. I hope you had fun."

"We did." He glanced over his shoulder at his friends. Brent was clapping Liam on the shoulder, while the other two gathered up their towels and stuff. "It was kind of cool hanging with Liam. He's a smart kid, you know?"

I flashed back to Cait's vision, and her theory about why it had actually been a good one. Was it just Cheerful Cait putting her happy spin on things as usual? Or was I really destined to see only doom and gloom in my visions?

Whatever. I could worry about that later. Because right now, I was way too aware that Megan was sort of giggling and sidling away, leaving me with Brayden. Obvious much? I just hoped he didn't notice.

But I also felt a flash of gratitude to her for doing it. It was nice to have friends.

WE WERE ALL pretty quiet on the ride home. Mom was in a good mood, which I guessed meant she and Mrs. March had hit it off. It was definitely a good thing that she was making friends, too; maybe it would help her chill out about stuff.

It took a few trips to bring in all the empty containers and leftover food from the car. But finally Cait and I dropped the last couple of loads on the counter, and Mom shooed us off.

"I'll put everything away," she said. "Happy birthday, girls."

"Thanks, Mom," Cait said, and I nodded.

Back in our room, Cait flopped onto her bed. "That was fun, right?" she said.

"Beyond fun." I flashed to Brayden and smiled.

"But without our visions, maybe it wouldn't have gone so well."

She sat up immediately. "Wait. Are you actually accepting that our visions might be, you know, not horrible?"

"No," I responded quickly. Then I paused. "Maybe. I don't know. I mean, a lot of our visions seem pretty pointless, you know? Like the one I had about Ms. Xavier, or the random ones we sometimes get from people we don't even know. It's annoying not knowing which ones are superimportant and which ones we can ignore."

"I know what you mean. Like, it would've been easy to ignore a vision of Megan playing with Amigo, right? Definitely random."

"Only not." I tried not to think about what could have happened. "And we could have ignored the Bianca ones, since they didn't have anything to do with us."

"Only not," Cait echoed. "Those visions were important even if they weren't what we thought."

"I guess." I wandered over and stared at myself in the mirror over the dresser. "Important or not, though—how are we supposed to know the difference?"

"I don't know. And I think the only way we can figure that out is with help from our grandmother. We need to try to find her somehow."

"I agree. Let's get on that—tomorrow, okay? I'm worn out." I dug into my purse for my favorite lip balm, but it wasn't there. "Oops," I said, vaguely remembering that I'd used it on the way home. "I'll be right back—I think I left something in the car."

I hurried for the front door. As I passed the kitchen, I could hear Mom humming as she cleaned up. She was in such a good mood today. Should Cait and I take advantage of that, maybe try talking to her right now? Or would that ruin what was supposed to be a happy day?

As I pondered that, I opened the door and stepped outside. A car was pulling up to the curb in front of our house. No, not a car—a taxi.

Huh? I hadn't seen a yellow cab since leaving San

Antonio. This particular taxi had the name of an Austin cab service printed on the side. What was it doing way out here in Aura?

The door swung open, and a woman climbed out. She was tall and angular, impeccably dressed in an expensive-looking burgundy suit. Her steel-gray hair was pulled back in a sleek bun, and her face wore an expression only slightly less haughty than you might expect from the Queen of England.

I squinted at her, trying to figure out why she looked so familiar. Just then Mom appeared in the doorway with Caitlyn right behind her.

"Cassie, I was telling Cait we should—" Mom cut herself off with a loud gasp.

The gray-haired woman heard her and turned to peer at us. Mom took a deep breath and pushed past me.

"Verity?" she called out, her voice shaking slightly. "Is that really you? Long time no see."

The woman came toward us. "Hello, Deidre," she said icily. "Yes, it has been some time, hasn't it?" Speaking of the Queen of England, the woman kind of sounded like her, too, with a distinct British accent of the upper-crust variety.

I gulped, suddenly realizing why she looked familiar. I'd seen her in my vision. And I was starting to get an inkling of who she might be and what this might mean. . . .

"Hello, girls," the woman went on, turning her clear blue eyes on Cait and me. "Happy birthday. I did get the day correct, didn't I?"

"Y-yes?" Caitlyn said uncertainly. "But who . . ."

The woman came closer, peering at us curiously. "Oh, my, you really are nearly identical, aren't you? So which of you is Caitlyn and which is Cassandra?"

"Girls," Mom broke in grimly before we could respond. "I suppose I should introduce you to Mrs. Verity Lockwood. Your grandmother."

My mouth fell open. "Grandmother?"

"*Lockwood?*" Cait squeaked out.

We traded a stunned look. *Wow!* And just when we thought our birthday couldn't get any more interesting!